Welcome To The Day

By Keven Renken

*To Betty –
Please read in good health!*

Keven Renken

Published By
Breaking Rules Publishing

Copyright 2019, Keven Renken

All Right Reserved.

All rights reserved. No part of this book may be reproduced stored in a retrieval system or transmitted in any form or by any means without the prior written permission of the publisher, except by the review who may quote brief passages in a review to be printed in a newspaper, magazine or journal.

The author has used the Breaking Rules Publishing editing services to edit this book.

Soft Cover – 10109
Published by Breaking Rules Publishing
St Petersburg, Florida
www.breakingrulespublishing.com

ACKNOWLEDGEMENTS

I must start with my mother, who must have recognized something in her skinny, timid middle child and saved every single thing he put down on paper. Years later these boxes of early writings would remind the middle-aged me of who I was and always will be - a writer. She knows, wherever she is, that she may very well have saved my life.

I started writing this novel, onstage, when I was in a play. It was a couple years after my mother's death, and I was playing a writer, and being all method-y, I thought that if I was on stage and the scene wasn't focused on my character, that I would have a notebook with me and I would be writing. The name of the theatre company and the man who cast me and directed the show are now lost to the sands of time (I only remember the name of the play - The Shadow Box by Michael Cristofer) but I want to thank him anyway. The actual physical process of writing this began then.

I took Melissa Carroll's class Narration and Description at the University of South Florida, and she sparked in me the desire to write again after a very long hiatus, so I owe her a huge debt. Also, thanks to Michael Staczar for telling me about the creative writing program at the University of Tampa, and to the mentors who helped me through that program - Josip Novakovich, Corinna Vallianatos, Jessica Anthony and Alan Michael Parker. A special thanks to Erica Dawson and Lynne Bartis, who have a special talent for nurturing artists. I have way too many friends to thank by name, but I especially want to mention Jose Gelats, Bruce Hardin, Ike McMahon and David Fox, who buoy me up with laughter and wit and love.

Last, but not least, I want to thank my family – especially my older sister and my father. Their presence is felt keenly throughout this work.

And Bill. Always Bill. Forever Bill. He is the best part of me.

CHAPTER 1

First there was the dreaming, and in the dream Raymond Chandler – named for the writer of a book on a shelf in the room where he was born – was once again on a tractor and towing a plow as it churned the earth into dark clouds as he drove towards the sky. At the other end of the field, Joanne was standing in front of a pickup truck and waving at him. She wore a dress patterned with flowers of many colors. His body hummed with the vibrations of the tractor as he chugged his way towards her. The vibrations begin to hurt, a hurt that would last until today, and that dream was over but the dreaming continued because he rolled over in bed and Joanne was lying there, in the same dress, looking at him. Those eyes. So blue. He would say that and she would ask "How blue? What kind of blue?" And he would have no words. One time he said it was the same blue as in Joe's crayons and she turned away from him. "Oh Raymond," she said, shaking her head. There was a sound in her voice he had heard before. After a while he stopped mentioning the color of her eyes.

    She only used his whole first name when she really wanted to say a lot more words to him instead. But that morning she was there and looking at him, those eyes glancing back and across his face, reminding herself, maybe, of what he looked like. She was smiling. "Good morning Ray," she said. "Welcome to the day." So only "Ray" today. She used to wake their children that way. Welcome to the day. He would hear it down the hall when he himself was still yawning and stretching, the sun from the glass doors leading to the backyard spilling onto the hardwood floor in their bedroom, creating long rectangles of light. Welcome to the day. Like a greeter at church. He would close his eyes again – waking up to sunshine meant he had overslept anyway, which he never did, so why not now? But she said it again and that time her voice was close. He would open his eyes and see her standing in the doorway, her arms on her hips, looking at him. She would smile. "Welcome to the day."

Said a third time, but this time almost a question, as if he had a choice. Then she would turn and go down the hall, and in her wake he would smell the bacon already frying in the kitchen.

So he could say her eyes were blue like bacon smelled good, but she would only laugh, not getting what he meant. Today there was no smell of bacon, and there she was, in bed still, which was not the usual routine. Her eyes, so blue, were searching his face. For what? He reached out to touch her face, but stopped. Something was not right. He studied her features for something he didn't recognize. It was all so familiar. The forehead, broad and high. He would often say because it was full of brains, a statement that would produce a dismissive "Huh" from her before she would turn back to her work. Her nose, maybe a little long and angular for the roundness of her face – though early in their courtship when physical contact did not make him awkward, he would lean in to kiss her but press his face against hers first, as if kissing was a two-step process. He would feel her nose against his cheek. So from that moment, when he could feel her skin against his, the texture and character of it, the touch of her nose triggered a feeling in his chest, his heart beating faster than it usually did. This changed the longer they knew each other. He would no longer lean in and press his face against hers before going in for a kiss. The kisses, when they came, were pecks on the cheek, the forehead. Or a quick grazing on the lips. Contact with the nose was with his fingers. He would look at her and something familiar would happen, a quickness now reduced to a fluttering. But he would smile and reach out and touch the tip of her nose with his finger. Then he would feel the blood rise in his cheeks. But not before he saw her smile back.

So the forehead. The nose. The eyebrows which remained dark even after her brown hair, brushed back off her face in delicate waves, was laced with grey. The cheeks ruddy and pink as if windblown. The lips, narrow and pulled down at the corners but quick to spring upwards into a smile. And those eyes. The color of.

"Good morning." She smiled. "Welcome to the day…" He smiled back. He reached out to touch her face. And then his eyes were open and the dreaming was done.

"… Dad."

He blinked. Blinked again. Her voice was coming from behind him now. But it was no longer her. He turned over, the bones in his shoulder rubbing together in protest.

The room was bathed in light. He looked at the pale green walls – a color his daughter had insisted upon because it was neither too feminine nor too masculine – and the white molding around the door and windows that the daughter had spent hours painting because every time she tried to help he got color all over the walls and floor. He scanned the room, taking silent inventory of the furniture. The nightstand with lamp, clock that read 7:06, copy of Readers Digest from three months ago. Chest of drawers, bureau. Family pictures on the wall, many of them including Joanne.

And there she was, standing in the doorway, his daughter, arms crossed over her chest. Hair not in brown and grey curls like her mother but yellow like straw and pulled back tight off her face and hanging down her neck. The look made her ears seem large. The nose thinner and longer. The lips thinner too, and the edges of her mouth curving down. The face was full and fleshy. She uncrossed her arms and the thumb and pinky on her right hand reached over to her left hand and rotated the wedding ring she wore.

"Welcome to the day, Dad." She said it again then turned her left wrist to look at her watch. "Remember, you have a doctor's appointment at nine. And I still have to get Joey to school. We've got a lot to do today, so don't dawdle." The right hand went back to the left and continued rotating the wedding ring, and she turned and shuffled down the hall out of view, her slippers brushing against the floor as she walked.

Dawdle. He lingered on the word for a moment. What an odd sound the word made when you said it. He whispered the word over and over, listening to the way it sounded as it came out of his mouth. Dawdle. He turned his head, though he already knew no one was in bed beside him. She certainly didn't dawdle – in fact, everyone seemed to be in a hurry this morning. His wife in the quickness of his dreams. His daughter when getting on with her day.

The bones in his shoulder ached in protest as he sat up in bed. He needed to remember to take something for that, though he also knew his daughter would take care of it for him, laying his morning pills out at his place at the table, arranging them in order by size, smallest to largest. He had to get his gag reflex working before he could tackle the larger ones. Some of them were as big as a small child his wife used to say, only half exaggerating.

His wife. He smiled as he looked over on the side of the bed where a minute before he had imagined her. He ran his hand over the pillowcase, also pale green. The pillow was made out of something called memory foam, which he had found funny. Foam that had a memory. He pushed down on the pillow with his finger and the imprint stayed for several seconds before relaxing into its original shape. He pushed again, harder and deeper this time. That imprint also eventually disappeared. It was, after all, just foam. There was no memory here. There hadn't been for a very long time.

He swung his legs around so his feet would touch the floor, his nails scraping against the hard wood. He needed to ask Cassie to help him trim his nails. Of course, if the rug was still there...After his left leg became unreliable, buckling under his weight without warning, Cassie flew into a frenzy, stomping around the house yanking every loose rug off the floor and hauling them off to Goodwill. He shook his head when she did it, but before long he was walking around without shoes or socks, feeling the coolness of the wood on the calluses of his toes. This further angered his daughter, who took to following him around the house with his slippers in her hands, speaking to him in a voice pitched high in her register. She was almost impossible to ignore once that voice came into play.

He sat for a minute, rubbing his feet on the floor. The moisture hung in the air, thick and stifling like a blanket. His synthetic pajama shirt still clung to his back with sweat. He had been here almost a year and he still couldn't get used to how hot it got. The heat pushed against his chest, making him take short, shallow breaths. It hurt. At first he was against moving here. He claimed it was hotter in the city. But it really wasn't about the heat. He had fallen again – this time while trying to mow the yard by the road outside his house – and hit his head on the asphalt. He couldn't get up until a neighbor drove by ten minutes later. This time she spent money she didn't have to pack up the house and move him into town with her. And there was that voice, that upper register, and you would promise anything to make it stop.

So here he was, a country man in the city, where it was so hot he couldn't breathe. Where he heard traffic when he couldn't sleep, even though they were at least a mile from any major highway. Where he couldn't see stars in the night sky because of the lights from the city. Where his only living child could not speak to him without using the upper register, reminding him almost every day that she was irritated. At him perhaps, though most anything brought on the voice these days. Most mornings he would wrap his resolve around him like a blanket and he could still barely feel the daily onslaught poking at him, into him. He sat for a moment longer, trying to breathe deep.

"Dad!"

There it was.

"If you want any breakfast, you gotta get up now!"

Breakfast. Of course. He listened to the sounds from the kitchen, identifying each one. The percolating of the coffee pot. The sound the toaster made when she pushed the bread down. The sizzling as she fried the eggs. And of course the shuffling as she moved from one task to another. Brush, brush, brush stop. Brush, brush, brush stop. Everything was just a few steps from every other thing in her kitchen.

He sighed. It was all so familiar. The sounds. The smells that went along with it. The voice. His daughter's face as she used that voice. Even the doctor. It was both too much and not enough. He needed something new and surprising to give him enough energy to stand up. He looked over his shoulder at the bed. Of course, nothing. But seeing her, even for a few seconds, was enough. Enough for now.

One deep breath, and as he exhaled he pushed himself up off the bed, his arms shaking until he was upright. He looked down at his feet and wiggled his toes. Oh yes. Those nails. He must speak to Cassie about those nails. That would make the upper register kick in for sure.

One small step forward on his left leg, the leg that couldn't be trusted. He had to be careful or he would fall again, and then the whole day would descend into chaos. Had to be careful or Cassie would unleash a litany of worry that he had unknowingly heaped upon her with his failing body. One more small step. All seemed to be well today, at least so far. Nonetheless he kept his eyes on his feet and held onto the wall for support as he slowly padded through the door and down the hallway into the kitchen.

CHAPTER 2

God damn it.
She put her finger into her mouth, the finger with the wedding ring on it. At the same time, she half turned to the doorway to the kitchen. He was not standing there. She turned back around, and with the finger still in her mouth, whispered another one.
Motherfucker.
She peeked over her shoulder again. He still wasn't there. She took the finger out of her mouth and shook her whole hand, as if the pain would fly off of her finger into the air. She took the handle of the skillet with her other hand, and put the left one back in her mouth. She walked over to the head of the table with the skillet, but then turned and went back to the stove. The spatula was right there. Now she needed both hands, so she took the left one out of her mouth and

gingerly picked up the spatula. Back at the table, she dumped the eggs onto his plate. The yolk of one broke, and the yellow spread over the plate. He was not going to like that. He liked to break the yolks with his toast.

    Today felt off, like she was missing seconds and then going back to reclaim them. She had done this for so long that usually every step is done from rote memory and no step is wasted. Not this morning. She was expecting a phone call and even though it was still early, the anticipation was distracting her. She started the coffee pot without changing the grounds, and the coffee, for some reason, ran onto the counter. A process that should have taken one minute ten seconds actually took twice as long. She let the skillet sit on the stove without turning the burner on until after the coffee catastrophe had played itself out. And now the splatter of oil burning her finger. She held it up to the light without looking for her glasses. A tiny spot, even smaller than a dime, was a deep red on the side of the finger. Butter they say. Butter is supposed to be good for a burn. She went to the refrigerator to open it and then stopped. The butter should have been out already.

    Toast. There should be toast. Shit.

    She opened the fridge and grabbed the

bread before remembering the burn on her finger. She swore again – son of a bitch – and the half loaf of white slipped out of her hand and fell to the floor. She simply stood and stared at it, putting her finger back in her mouth. She listened to her heartbeat. Sounded a little fast. She turned her hearing out to the house. No sound from Joey's room, which wasn't a surprise. That one would take multiple trips to rouse. Some shuffling from Dad's room. Sounded like socks. No slippers. She looked around her. The slippers weren't in the kitchen – which meant they were with him and he was not using them.

    Again.

    Speaking of pushing buttons. She bent over and picked up the still wrapped loaf and carried it over to the counter. She reached into the bag past the heel – Dad didn't like the heel – and took two pieces that she popped in the toaster. She pushed down the handle and then checked the knob on the side. She turned it to 4 – Dad also liked his toast dark. It should take a little more than a minute. She leaned against the counter and did a quick survey. To her right the coffee percolated – no dark liquid spread across the counter this time. To her left the smell of bread toasting was in the air. Down the counter to her right the offending skillet was resting, handle to one side, in the sink. In front of her, down at the other end of the kitchen, the table was set for her father and her son. Plates, silverware, napkin, coffee cup, glasses...

There was no orange juice. He liked his glass of orange juice. Fuck.

She pushed herself off from the counter and opened the refrigerator in three steps. The juice was behind the milk behind the diet soda which she never drank. It was in front of everything else, however, because Joey came in at odd times, reached in and drank straight from the bottle. He would tilt his head back, and she'd watch his Adam's apple move as he took several deep swallows. Holding the bottle in front of him, he would pause, wait, and then belch, a deep, loud resonant sound which was, more often than not followed by "This tastes like shit. And it's flat." Her dad, sitting at the table reading the paper as if he were memorizing lines in a play, would look up and glare at Joey over his glasses. "Watch the cussing," he'd say before looking back down at his paper. He would spend the next several seconds looking over the print as if he couldn't remember where he was reading. Joey would shrug his shoulders and shove the bottle back into the fridge before belching a second time, softer this time but more drawn out and walk out of the kitchen with his head down, his bare feet slapping the floor with each step. Her family dynamic in one moment.

    She scanned the countertop, the table, even the top of the fridge. Her cigarettes were nowhere to be found. She played with the wedding ring on her left hand. Another break in the routine – usually she had her morning smoke by now. One step out onto the back porch, close the door, and for about two minutes, as she pulled smoke into her lungs and held it there, estimating the considerable damage of each second, her mind was quiet. She did not calculate mistake, contemplate failure, or pine for what could have been but wasn't. But this morning it hasn't happened, and nothing was going right. She scanned again. No cigarettes, but her cell phone was an arms-length away. She picked it up, opened the back door and stepped out to the porch. She looked at the pool that husband number two seemed to think they could not live without. She would have to remind Joey to brush it after school. The morning was clear and hot – she could feel the moisture on her face in a few seconds. Or maybe that was lack of a cigarette that was making her break out into a sweat. She inhaled and held, almost as a reflex, wishing she were taking in nicotine. This morning it was only fresh air.

    She exhaled, listening to her breath as it left her mouth. It was quiet if she could hear herself breathe. She inhaled again, and turned to look back into the house. The back door was two panes of glass and she could see the whole kitchen. But she looked at her reflection instead. Some days she didn't recognize the person looking back at her – today was one of those days. She had never had great skin – but when did it get so dry and lined? She exhaled and reached up to touch her face, and saw the reflection of her hand do the same thing. Her cheeks were so round, almost chubby. There was a day when she had fine, high cheekbones that pointed down to her full mouth and a nice prominent jaw line that led to a fine point of a chin – now she could barely tell where her jaw line was. Her face seemed to go down into her neck and then into her collar. She ran her fingers along the lines that went to the edges of her mouth and actually seemed to pull it at the corners. She read in a medical journal at work once that they were called nasolabial folds. Her third husband, claiming they were adorable, called them laugh lines. If that was indeed what they were called, then she was most definitely not amused. She used the fingers of both hands to pull the skin on each side of her face back towards her ears. The folds were gone but the lines were still visible. And it made her mouth look weird, stretched out more than it should be across her face.

    She let go and watched her face settle back into itself as she exhaled. She checked her phone quickly – no call yet - before leaning into the glass and looking into the reflection of her eyes as she inhaled again. There were lines around and under her eyes, but at least they were not bloodshot. The pupils were still a brilliant blue, even after all these years. The better to see you with, my dear. That was in a book she had read to Joey once, and he loved it so much that he asked her to say it again and again. The better to see you with my dear. That made her smile, and she watched the skin of her face light up with a network of lines in every conceivable location. Well, not the nose itself. Or the cheeks. Because they were fat cheeks. She exhaled, imagining the smoke as it left her mouth and scattered into the air.

    Smoke. She saw real smoke.
    But it wasn't coming from her mouth.

Instead she saw smoke, through the glass, in the kitchen, wispy and gray, rising out of the toaster.

Shit.

She shoved her phone back into her pants pocket with one hand as she opened the back door with the other and walked over to the toaster in seven steps. With a ferocity that she didn't even know she had, she yanked the chord out of the wall socket, picked up the toaster with both hands and flipped it and shook it over the marble countertop. Black crumbs flew everywhere. One piece of toast, dark as coal, fell to the ground but the other refused to budge. She continued to shake the errant appliance, saying shit, shit, shit, again and again, as if the very act of repetition would dislodge it. No such luck. The springs inside made a metallic clang as she set it back on the counter. She leaned over the machine and reached in for the offending bread. She touched the burn on her left hand to the wires on the inside, and reared back in pain. She stood for a second in the middle of the kitchen, shaking her hand and listening to herself panting. This was just too much.

"Dad!" If you want any breakfast, you gotta get up now!"

She listened and after a few seconds

she heard him moving around again. He would not be happy. She looked down to the floor and regarded the crumbs and burned piece of toast that flew out of her hands seconds before. Hearing a sound, she looked up just in time to see him shuffling through the doorway to the kitchen. He was holding onto the walls as he moved. He paused for a second and they regarded each other.

"It smells like smoke in here." He looked her in the eye as he said this. "I smell smoke."

"Yeah I know. Well..." she shrugged and gestured helplessly to the carnage on the floor. They had done this dance before. Some mornings he had caught her before she was done with her "cancer sticks" (as he had called them), or commented on the smell on her breath or clothes while she was serving him breakfast. Today it was his food, though she still felt like the smell clung to her, permeating her skin. She bent down and picked up the crumbs by hand, even though there was a dust-buster mere feet away in a cabinet. It was just easier not to look at him sometimes.

The shuffling began again, and she looked out of the corner of her eyes to watch him. Sitting himself down was an elaborate enterprise. He would hold onto the edge of the table with his left hand, turn his body slowly to one side as if he were going to ride the chair side saddle, slowly bend his knees until his ass touched the seat, and turn his whole body to face forward, crossing his free hand over his body to help move the weak left leg. It looked choreographed. It made her wince as she watched it. She turned away and concentrated on the floor, scanning for every possible piece of evidence of her earlier folly. When she was satisfied she had gotten it all, she stood, using the edge of the counter for support.

"I could make you some more toast if you want." There was no answer. She looked over to see him sitting with his fingers interlocked in front of the messy eggs and his head bowed. His lips were moving, saying silently the prayer she had heard a million times as a child:

Come Lord Jesus be our guest
And let these gifts to us be blessed.
Amen.

Or at least that's how she thought it went. Once she learned it, she rattled it off quickly without thinking about it, as if that meant she would get to eat quicker. After a while it just sounded like sounds to her, sounds that meant nothing. This time she mouthed the words with him and tried to think about what she was saying. "And let these gifts to us be blessed" sounded awkward and turned around. She waited for him to open his eyes before she spoke again.

"I said, do you want more toast? Since I burned the last batch?"

"Huh?" He blinked at her. His eyes didn't register on her face for a while. Then he squinted. "What?

"Toast. I said! Do you want more toast!" She heard the pitch of her voice rising.

"Oh. Sure." He looked down at his plate. "Even though…" He left the rest of the sentence unspoken.

"Okay then" She went back to the counter and popped two more slices in the toaster, being very careful to turn the knob down to three this time. "So you have your eggs. And your juice. And coffee…" Her heart beat faster for a second, but she looked behind her, and saw the coffee pot still percolating. "You'll have your coffee in a second…" She turned back around. He was already eating. This too looked choreographed. He cut the egg with his fork, speared it and held it up over the plate where he let the yellow run off. Then he stuck the fork in his mouth and tilted his head to one side, as if he were listening to himself slowly chew. She could hear his teeth click from across the kitchen, so maybe he was.

She continued the breakfast inventory. "Now if I could only get that son of mine off his ass and in the kitchen to eat some breakfast..."

"Watch the cussing," her father droned. She ignored him and strode to the kitchen doorway in six steps. She grabbed hold of both sides of the door as if she were Samson pushing down the pillars in the temple. Her voice slid effortlessly up to its upper register. "Hey! Joseph! If you don't get out of bed right this second..."

From the depths of the hallway a muffled voice, probably buried deep in a pillowsleepily responded. "Jesus Christ, Mom..."

"Watch the...," her father began again.

"...why do you have to be so loud in the morning?"

"I'm loud all the time! Now get the hell in here and eat some breakfast right this instant!" She let go of the doorway and walked over to the cabinets to get two coffee cups.

Her father looked up at her, opened his mouth, paused, and shoved a forkful of eggs into his mouth. As she poured the coffee, the toast sprang up, nice and brown this time. From the hallway a door opened and slammed shut, and she heard the padding of feet down the hallway and through the living room into the kitchen. She turned to the refrigerator to get the butter and saw her only child standing in the doorway. Christ he looked a mess. He wore his hair long so you couldn't see his forehead, ears or the back of his neck. Today it was flat on one side and stuck out in many directions on the top and the other side. A plain blue T-shirt and blue jeans that were at least three sizes too big so that they showed the top of his boxers also looked as if they had been left in the dryer. One of his thin white arms was bent at the elbow as he rubbed his eyes with his hand.

"Did you sleep in your clothes again?" She asked. She winced at the harsh sound of her own voice.

"So?" He plodded over to the left of his grandfather and sat down, putting both his head in his hands. "So what if I did?" He continued rubbing his eyes, as if waking. Her father, his mouth full of egg, looked over at him and continued chewing.

"Nothing. It just looks…" she searched for the right word. "Messy is all." She buttered the toast with even strokes, the knife making a scraping sound. "I suppose that's what you're wearing to school today."

"Uh." He looked up for the first time. "I was thinking maybe I was going to stay home from school today."

"What?" She turned sharply, the butter knife still in her hand.

"Mom, I, uh..." He searched for a lie. "I don't feel so good."

"Well you certainly look like shit!" She advanced towards him, gesturing with the butter knife, the plate of toast balanced in her other hand. Her voice was way up in its upper register.

"But 'I don't feel so good' is bullshit!" She slams the plate down in front of her father. He keeps his eyes on his eggs, and shovels more food into his mouth. His teeth click as he chews and he shakes his head slowly.

"Oh, Mom," Joey whined. His hands dart up to his face and his fingers rifled through the hair on his forehead. "I think I have a fever or something..."

"Let me see." She darted around her father, who quietly put a piece of toast in his mouth, to the other side of the table where her son sat. She practically slapped her hand onto his forehead. She held it there for a few seconds, staring at him the whole time. "You don't have a fever," she said finally, taking her hand down and shaking it like it were a thermometer. "Feels perfectly normal to me."

Joey's hand slid down to his Adam's apple. "And I have a sore throat."

"Oh just stop it! You are not sick! You just don't want to go to school!" She walked away from Joey and went around her father towards the fridge. As she did, she touched her father on the shoulder. The touch was gentle, which surprised her since she was not feeling particularly gentle this morning. She continued to the fridge and waited until she had her hand on the door handle before she turned back to address her son. "So..." she stared through him, "what do you want for breakfast?"

"Nothing. Ugghh..." He made a face before he bent over and put his head on the table and his arms on top of his hair. "I hate breakfast." He said to the floor.

"Hate," she said as she opened the fridge and took out the creamer. She stirred the creamer into the cups of coffee still sitting on the counter, "Hate. Hmmmm... such a strong word."

"God, Mom," Joey said still to the floor. His grandfather wiped the yolk up with his last piece of toast and turned to him but said nothing. Cassie carried the two cups over to the table and set one down in front of her father. She sat down opposite her son and took a long sip from the cup. It wasn't a cigarette, but it would have to do. She felt the warmth go down her throat and looked over at her son's long curly hair. She had nothing else to say so she took another sip of coffee. She looked over at her father. He had finished his breakfast and pushed his plate away. The silverware was stacked upside down on top of the plate, a thing he did for as long as she had known him. He was gripping his coffee cup with both hands and bent over almost to the edge of the cup before he tipped it to get coffee in his mouth. She closed her eyes and breathed. They would have to leave soon if they were going to get Joey to school and her father to the doctor. But right now she didn't want to move. She took another sip of coffee, her eyes still closed. It was quiet.

    She listened to herself breathe. And then she checked her phone.

CHAPTER 3

The heavy glass doors slid open of their own accord as the trio approached. Cassie took big steps, strode with a purpose, but she paused when the automatic doors do their thing. She was never quite convinced it will happen, and she waited instead of running into her own reflection. Shuffling behind her and to one side, breathing heavily, was her father. He leaned far to one side, leaned hard on his cane. Behind her was Joey. His feet, shoved into sneakers that were white five years ago and trailing untied shoelaces like umbilical cords, were certainly moving, though the rest of him was rigor mortis, rigid and unyielding. His hands were shoved wrist deep into his jean pockets and his shoulders were hunched up to his neck like he's cold – or maybe his head was sunk down and thrust forward as if he were a turtle. They make a fine group.

    She stepped through and glanced over her shoulder to make sure the other two made it through. She turned and surveyed the waiting room, taking a deep breath as she did so. Hospitals always smelled so antiseptic and clean, a level of sanitation she could never seem to accomplish in her own home. No matter how hard she tried, no matter how much she scrubbed and sprayed, she could never get it as clean, or at least as clean-smelling as a hospital. And regardless of the effort, her tousled-hair son would come in after and effectively piss all over it. Making a hacking sound, he proclaimed his displeasure loud enough for the whole house to hear. "Jesus Christ! Did Grandpa puke here?" Before she could even reply he stomped out and down the hall to his room, slamming his door to further make his point. She would stand in the middle of the room, looking after him for a long time. Finally she would sigh, go under the kitchen sink to get the cleaning supplies and begin again.

    Speaking of puke...Something was definitely off today. That clean antiseptic smell that she loved so much was not there. She looked over in the direction of her son and her father. Joey had already dropped himself down into a waiting room chair and was in the process of putting buds into his ears, his phone clutched so firmly in his hand his knuckles were white. Dad had his back to her, sliding his feet slowly across the floor, placing the cane in front of him with each step. A movement out of the corner of her eye caught her attention. She turned to watch an orderly, dressed in white, his arms the size of sides of beef, mop a puddle of brown liquid off the floor. She stood and watched him. His bald head, shiny and dark as chocolate, was bent towards the floor. There was a rhythm to the way he moved, as if he didn't have to think about what he was doing, making long swipes across the floor with the mop.

"Jesus, Grandpa!!"

Her attention shot back over to her family. Her father was falling, his body turned sideways as he went down. Joey had bolted to his feet, the buds still in his ears and the phone gripped in his hand, but he stood still, not moving forward to help his grandfather. Her mouth opened but no sound came out. She jerked forward, but she didn't feel herself actually travel to his side. Suddenly she was just there, bent over him as he lie curled into himself on the floor.

"What the hell! Dad! Are you okay?"

For a change, the curse word got no response from the old man. He didn't even look at her. Instead his eyes were half closed like he were concentrating on his own breaths, breaths that were hard and fast and raspy. She touched his shoulder, thin and bony and sticking up into the air and his arm, the one he landed on, reached across his body. He put his hand over hers and held on. She looked up at her son who still stood frozen by his chair.

"Joey!" No response. His eyes were wide and focused on his grandfather.

"JOEY!!" She waited for a second. Joey blinked once and then twice, his eyes finally focusing on his mother's face. With her free arm she waved him over.

"Get over here and help me with your grandfather." She hoped her voice sounded calm since anything else would have the equivalent effect of making sharp, jerking movements in the direction of a wild animal. Joey would flee from the situation, and right now she needed all the help she could get. She braced her legs – lift with your knees, she thought – and put her purse down on the floor before reaching under the old man's arm to help him up. He was making small waving motions in front of himself with both his hands and was being absolutely no help whatsoever.

And suddenly the orderly was there. More gently than she would have expected from such a large man, he got down on his knees on the other side of her fallen father and with both hands nudged him into a sitting position. Without letting go of her dad's shoulder, the orderly stood in front of him, put his other arm under the old man's legs and picked him up off the floor. Cassie stood back and looked at the unusual tableau, a large brown-skinned man with muscles holding an old frail man in his arms as if he was about to carry him across the threshold. Dad leaned into the man's chest like he was being cradled. His hands had stopped moving – one hung down limply behind the orderly's back and the other one lay curled in his lap.

"You want me to get someone?" The orderly stood with her father in his arms.

"I'm sure he's fine. He does that sometimes." She looked at the orderly's arms. The muscles flexed beneath his skin.

"You want a wheelchair? I could get you a wheelchair."

"No. That's okay. Just put him over there." She gestured over to the bank of chairs where Joey was slowly sitting back down. "Like I said, I'm sure he'll be fine. He falls, we get him back up. He falls again. It's this thing we do." The orderly scanned her face, no doubt wondering if she were joking. Several seconds passed, and then he nodded his head.

"Okay." He carried her father over to the chairs. "But I really could get you a wheelchair. If he falls over a lot, maybe he should use a wheelchair."

She flinched. He thought she was an unfit daughter. Or at least didn't know what was best for her own flesh and blood. She hurried after the orderly as he carried her father over to the banks of chairs where Joey sat, wanting to look helpful. All she could see of her father was the one skinny sleeved arm dangling behind the orderly's broad back, and his equally thin legs. They almost bounced as the orderly carried him. Dad was wearing grey tennis shoes, something he never did before moving in with her – at least never before that she could think of. A small pink wad of gum was stuck to the bottom of one shoe.

The orderly had made it to the chairs and was standing next to Joey, who had already gone back to listening to his music and didn't even look up at the big man standing over him with his grandfather in his arms. The music was so loud that she could hear it as she approached the group, though she had no idea who was singing. They never talked music, she and her son. Evidently the orderly knew it though, because he began humming the melody as he bent over and oh-so- gently – again, such gentleness in such a big man - placed the old man in the chair next to Joey. The orderly smiled and tapped Joey on the shoulder. The teenager jerked as if electrocuted when the big man touched him, then looked up to stare in the man's face.

"Nice tunes, man." The orderly continued smiling, displaying a mouth of perfect, straight white teeth. He chuckled at the teenager. "Sorry man, didn't mean to scare you." Joey took one bud out and held it away from his ear as he continued looking at the big man's face. The music got louder and spilled out into the waiting room. Cassie could hear it even better though she still had no idea who the singer was.

"I said nice tunes." The orderly leaned over and spoke directly into Joey's face, talking louder as if Joey was deaf. "I got them on rotation too. Do you know..." He mentioned a group that, to Cassie's ears, sounded like gibberish. Joey shook his head slowly. The orderly reached into his pocket and brought out his phone and began running his thumb across the screen. Finding what he was looking for, he held the phone, screen out, to Joey. But the teenager had already dropped his gaze to his own portable electronic device, put the bud back in his ear and was nodding slowly to the music which seemed to emanate from him like a force field. The orderly hesitated for a moment, his arm still holding his phone out to Joey. Cassie stepped forward and touched the orderly's arm.

"That's my son. Loves himself some music. Actual conversation with other human beings...not so much." She moved herself further into the orderly's line of vision and extended the hand that wasn't gripping her cell phone. "Hi there. Cassie here. Thank you so much for helping me with Dad."

The orderly took her hand and shook energetically. The squeeze on her fingers almost hurt it was so firm. "Bennie. And not a problem. Didn't mind at all. Hey..." he shrugged, his big mitt of a hand still wrapped around hers. "It's in the job description. I just hope he's okay. Didn't hurt himself, or have a medical...issue or whatever."

"No." Cassie stood there wondering if she should pull her hand away or shake it again. His holding onto it had now officially reached the awkward stage. "Like I said, he falls sometimes. Got a weak leg." Bennie let go of her hand and she pointed over at her father, who had sunk back into the chair and was staring ahead of him (though was he listening to Joey's music? It kind of looked like he was). "Hence the cane."

Bennie laughed. "Yeah, I guess so. Makes sense." He gestured over to his bucket and mop and the brown puddle of liquid that smelled like vomit. "Well, I better get back to work. Nice to meet you Cassie. If there's anything else I can help you with, just let me know." He gestured again. "I'll be right over there...cleaning up."

Cassie waved him off. "Nah, I think we're good. But thanks. And thanks again. For helping with my father."

"Anytime." Bennie nodded his head and turned to walk away. Cassie could hear him hum the tune from Joey's phone. She made a mental note to ask Joey what it was called. She went over to her sitting family. Her father was resting his head on his hand, which was resting on the edge of the chair. His wispy grey hair, which was usually so carefully combed and parted on the right, was splayed in every direction on his head. Joey was nodding his head to his music, his long legs spread out in front of him. As his mother approached he looked up and smiled.

"Damn Mom," he said, talking loudly enough that he could hear himself over his own music, "Flirt much?"

Cassie felt heat rise in her cheeks. "Flirt?" she said, also louder than was absolutely necessary. "What are you talking about?"

"The black guy. Cleaning up the barf." Joey gestured in the direction of Bennie, who was once more brushing his mop in long strokes across the floor. "The way you two were holding hands, I thought you'd dry hump right here on the floor. Don't give up the groceries quite yet, Ma. At least make him buy you dinner first." Joey was smiling, enjoying his own joke. "Keep your standards somewhat high for god's sake."

Cassie was smiling too. This joking around didn't happen often. "If I'd kept my standards high, I'd never have married your father." As soon as she said it, she regretted it. Something like a shadow passed over Joey's face and he stopped smiling. She had gone too far. She had relaxed into the moment, and that had tripped her up. And even though what she had said wasn't even close to true – marrying Joey's dad, husband number three, might have been the one right thing, besides Joey, that she had done with her life – she had thought, mistakenly, that they were in joke mode. Now she had lost her son, and it might be hours before he ventured back. Joey bent his head over his phone and turned up the music. It was so loud that Cassie could make out the lyrics.

    She looked around, wanting suddenly to make herself busy with someone. Over to the side of the room Bennie was putting his mop into his bucket for the last time, and was propping up a yellow WET FLOOR signs in the location of the vomit. She scanned the room, something she had done a million times before. The year before, the hospital had decided that white was too cold and uninviting and had renovated the waiting room. The powers that be had settled on a southwestern theme, which might have worked in New Mexico but was strangely out of place in Florida. The walls were a dark green bordered in a brown and orange pattern. Indian art hung on the walls and pottery sat on the tables, sharing space with Time and Newsweek magazine. No plants though, so nothing actually lived here. What would they have put here? Cactus? One stray child or infirm old person pricking themselves and that would have been that. So no plants. Just sick humans hanging out with images of horses and bows and arrows.

Her eyes made it to the receptionist desk. The woman sitting there actually looked like an Indian. Black hair parted severely in the middle and pulled back into a pony tail. Cassie remembered the hint of a mustache on the upper lip the last time she brought her dad here.

Checking in would have been good.

She walked over to the desk. Don't look at the mustache. Don't look at the mustache. Though by the time she got there her eyes were firmly trained in that direction. She had to clear her throat three times before she got The Mustache to look up.

"Hello, can I help you?" The Mustache said, looking past Cassie to the clock on the back wall. Cassie gave her Raymond's name, and The Mustache looked down at the computer squinting at the names as she scrolled through today's appointments. "Oh yes, here he is," she said, almost too fast. "The doctor is running late – he had an emergency. Just have a seat. We'll be with you as soon as we can." She looked up briefly, and she smiled so widely it threatened to break her face in half. Cassie stared at the mustache. The receptionist searched her face for 2.5 seconds. "K?" The smile stayed firmly in place. "Good." And the head was down again, the receptionist's eyes trained on the screen as if it held the secrets of the universe.

Cassie stared at the top of her head for several seconds. She backed away before heading back to her son and father. When she got within earshot, she said to herself, though loudly enough for her child to hear. "Thank you very much..." She paused. "Bitch." The last word had the desired effect on Joey, who though buried deep into his music reacted as if he'd been goosed, his eyes and mouth making large circles. Her father, however, was resting his face in his left hand, his mouth hidden by his palm. He didn't look up. She crouched down in front of him.

"Dad..." she began, too loudly it seemed, since he jerked his head up. He stared at her, his eyes wide. She took his wrist, which floated in front of his face and started again. With her other hand she reached up and smoothed down his hair. "Dad..." she focused into his eyes, willing him to look back. "Dad. We have to go now. I've got to get Joey to school..."

"School" being evidently the only other words that soaked through the alt rock universe soaking into Joey's ears, he immediately scrunched up his face.

"Mmmmmoooooommmm…"

"You," she took her hand down from her father's head and pointed at her son. "Shut up right now." She continued to focus in on her father. "Okay? We're going now but it's only fifteen minutes away. The doctor's running behind and I'll be back before you even go in." She paused, hoping it had sunk in. His eyes were blinking and bloodshot. She tried again. "Okay?"

He nodded. Still holding onto his wrist, she rested it in his lap before she let go. She heard her voice from just a few second ago. I'll be back. Again. I'll be back. She took a step away and sighed before reaching over and smacking her son on the shoulder. His mouth was in a firm line. "Come on." She pointed in the direction of the door. "Let's go. You're going to be late." Joey shot out of the chair and past her but she remained looking at her father for a few seconds before hurrying after her son. She focused on the mass of blonde hair as he hurried through the automatic glass doors. He used to let her comb that hair, curving his head into her body and smiling as she ran a brush through it. That hadn't happened lately however. Not for some years now. Now he simply jerked his head away any time she reached out for it. No touching allowed.

She made it through the door before she turned around to look back in the waiting room. Her son had made it to the car by now and was tugging on the door handle as if simply by shear will he could force it open. But she was looking back at Raymond. He was resting his head on his hand again. He looked so tired.

For just a second his eyes flickered up to see her in the sun. And then the door closed and she saw nothing but her reflection.

CHAPTER 4

Raymond watched the hands. The doctor had taken his pulse, his blood pressure, listened to his heart and looked down his throat and into his ears and now the hands were looking for something to do. He flipped through Raymond's chart, paused on some pages, and then skimmed through it again. He looked at the old man then, though Raymond had the distinct impression he was gazing at his left ear.

The doctor began to talk. Raymond heard a few of the words he said. The word "four" made it to his subconscious. Another word, "aggressive," landed squarely where it needed to in the middle of his understanding. Another word, "months," seemed to circle around his head. But mostly he watched the man's hands. They were rough and red around the nails – they were working man's hands. Not a doctor's hands at all. They were folded by this time, on the open file. But they were not at rest. The fingers would flex out before coming back into the fold. Flex, flex, rest. Flex, flex, rest. It had a rhythm to it. The doctor obviously wanted to gesture.

"Of course you have options." A whole sentence broke through the fog in Raymond's brain. "There are always options." A huge pause. "Until there aren't anymore."

"What?" Raymond shook his head. He pushed his glasses up with one hand and rubbed his eyes. "I'm sorry. What did you say?"

The doctor looked startled. "No...I'm sorry. I know it's a lot to take in. Are you okay?"

Raymond surprised himself by laughing at the question. The doctor leaned back and smiled himself, his face turning pink. The edges of his mouth twitched as if they had trouble staying up. Raymond nodded his head and chuckled again, but the chuckle changed a cough and Raymond bent over, his face in his lap as his body was wracked with the effort to breathe. The doctor was on his feet in an instant but did not come forward. Out of the corner of his eye Raymond could see the doctor looking intently at him, his eyes open slightly larger than normal.

The coughing subsided and the room was quiet except for Raymond's breathing. The doctor exhaled deeply as Raymond continued to rest his head in his lap. "Well I guess that answered that question, huh?" the doctor said, forcing a laugh after. Raymond sat to look at him and nodded. The doctor looked around like something was missing.

"Where is…? Your daughter. Shouldn't she be here?"

Raymond shrugged. He listened to his heart. "She was. She brought me here. But her son…She had to take him to school." He paused, feeling the tightness in his chest which now carried much more significance than he could have ever guessed. "You know how it is. Pulled in many directions at once."

"Boy, do I ever." The doctor shook his head and smiled. "Tell me about it. But really, you should have your family here. Don't you think?"

Raymond looked at the younger man. He ran the doctor's words over and over in his mind. "Boy" sounded oddly over-familiar to him, and then, in the very next moment, he had felt scolded. Boy. Don't you think?

Boy?

"Don't you think?" the doctor asked again, and Raymond looked up. This time it was his turn to be startled. The doctor was standing very close to him. He didn't remember him being that close. Raymond took off his glasses and rubbed his eyes again. He felt suddenly very tired. The doctor put his hand on the old man's shoulder.

"It's always good," the doctor said, his voice dropping very low, "I think. It's always good to have someone with you."

"Yes, I suppose it is." Raymond continued to rub his eyes. He could see his right hand holding the glasses resting in his lap. It was shaking.

"Do you have someone?" The doctor bent down so his face was directly in Raymond's line of vision. "Someone to come get you after we're done?"

Raymond lifted his head and put his glasses on, almost poking himself in the nostril with one of the earpieces. The doctor's eyes were darting back and forth across the old man's face as if the cancer were there instead of in his lungs. Everyone was studying him so intently today. One of the joys, or sorrows, of old age, he thought. Everyone watched you either too closely or not at all. There seemed to be no in between.

The thought made him smile, and the doctor stepped back and grinned also. "My daughter Cassie," Raymond said, using facial muscles he didn't know he had to keep the smile on his face. "She's coming to pick me up after she drops her son off at school."

"That's good. Very good." The doctor turned and walked back to his desk. He picked up Raymond's file and studied it intently. "I'll want to talk to her when she gets here." The action had a finality to it Raymond didn't like. He scanned through his memory to find something to keep the conversation going. "Options?" he said after a few seconds. "You said there were options?"

"Ah yes." The doctor put the file on his desk, still open. This time he took his glasses off. He gestured with it as he walked around the desk and sat on the edge of it facing Raymond. "As I said, there are always options. Yours are, I'm afraid, somewhat limited. Surgery is definitely not one of them. Given your age and the advanced stage of the cancer, that one comes off the table right away. We could always try some combination of chemotherapy and radiation treatment. We have had limited success with extending the patient's life. Of course, getting approval from the insurance company, once again given your age and the advanced nature of the cancer, might be..." he paused briefly and glanced around at the file before looking back up, "...an issue. And there is always the question of quality of life, though there are a number of medications we could try to help with that."

He paused again, and this time he coughed into his hand. Both hands had become very active again. He looked at Raymond for a second before continuing. "Of course..." he paused yet a third time, "...the other option, and the one I would personally recommend, is we keep you as comfortable as possible, and you..." fourth pause, "...you start to get your affairs in order."

Affairs in order.

Those three words had a solidness to them. They landed hard on Raymond's ears and stayed there. He blinked, feeling the words sink into the soft matter of his brain. Affairs in order. Affairs. In. Order. He continued to blink. His eyes stung though there were no tears. The doctor stood and came towards him and Raymond involuntarily flinched. He needed to start getting his affairs in order. The doctor rested his hand on Raymond's shoulder, and Raymond looked at it as if he had no idea where it came from.

"But we can talk more about all of this when your daughter gets here." His hand stayed on Raymond's shoulder and his voice took on the quality of someone who was whispering a secret in church. "We'll go over all of this with her again. Okay?" The doctor looked Raymond in the face. For the first time the old man noticed that the younger man's eyes were blue.

Like Joanne's.

"Okay?" the doctor asked again, and this time he shook Raymond's shoulder lightly. "We'll talk more about all of this when your daughter gets here. Okay?" Raymond nodded and pushed upwards, leaning hard on his cane. It was obviously time for him to leave. The doctor took hold of him under his arm and helped him up, hovering at his elbow while Raymond steadied himself on his feet. The younger man walked slowly at Raymond's side as they left the examining room and walked down the hall. The doctor was talking the whole time, no longer using his whispering in church voice. Raymond heard him, but listened to nothing he said. Instead he concentrated on the art on the walls, paintings in broad watercolor brushstrokes of Indians wrapped in colorful blankets standing next to tall, muscular, dark horses.

In every one the Indians were looking out at the artist as if they were having their photo taken. Only the horses looked away at the horizon. Only the horses seemed to know what was really important.

The hallway, painted a burnt orange, eventually opened into the wide expanse, and forest green, of the waiting room. In here they had earthen plates hanging on the walls and stone pots with dried plants sitting on small tables, as if they had no fear that infirm old men with canes would come along and knock them over. People sat in groups of twos and threes in the rows of chairs. It smelled like medicine that didn't taste good. The doctor ushered him over to the nearest chair and held onto his arm until Raymond had himself firmly seated. Keeping his arm on Raymond's shoulder, the younger man stepped in front of him and crouched down so he could be at eye level with the old man.

"I'll let Erica know you're waiting for your daughter. When she gets here, let Erica know and I'll have you come back for a few minutes so I can talk to her. Okay?" He certainly needed a lot of approval, Raymond thought as he nodded his head. The doctor smiled and removed his hand from Raymond's shoulder. "And don't worry..."he paused, and Raymond felt for the first time as if he had nothing else to say. "Don't worry," he repeated as Raymond stared at him, "we'll all talk then."

He hurried away and Raymond watched him as he retreated. He looked in his direction long after he could no longer see the white coat. Finally he turned and looked at the opposite wall at the clock. It was later than he'd thought. Much later. Cassie, in full flush, should really have been in the waiting room when he came out. He knew her routine pretty well by now. He looked around but saw her nowhere, though he did see her expression, worried and stressed and tired, in other faces. He turned back to the clock and watched the second hand move around the face. If she was running late, she would be in especially fine form when she finally got here. He could just hear the voice now. He closed his eyes and listened to the sound in the room that would soon be disrupted by his daughter. People were speaking in low voices. On a TV somewhere an announcer was talking about the latest shooting in another part of the country. The relative quiet was interrupted every once in a while by a woman's voice over the intercom calling for a doctor or the relative of a patient.

Time stretched out in front of him

without a beginning or an end. When he still farmed and drove the tractor and plow through the soil, turning it over and making it dark, time seemed to go on forever. Later in the summer it was the hoe attached to the tractor as he drove it through rows of lush green corn or soybeans, their leaves bending past the machinery as he drove over the hill and to the fence, where he would turn and drive back into the moment. He could do that forever.

 A scream snapped his eyes open – but it was not the scream of a middle-aged woman. He turned awkwardly in his seat, his shoulder aching, his chest hurting. Behind him was a chubby woman, brown hair chopped off at the shoulders. Her arms, flabby with fat, were restraining a boy of about four or five who was refusing to sit still in her lap. His blonde hair was the color of straw and his face was scrunched up into a long protracted bawl. He looked a lot like Joe, except that Joe never made that much noise and would sit and suffer in painful and noiseless silence.

 He looked a lot like Joe.
 Like Joe.
 The thought of his son took Raymond's breath away. That memory, stealthy and quick, had snuck up on him. He turned

back around, no longer able to look at the screaming infant. His eyes stinging, he looked up at the clock facing him on the wall. It was now a half hour later. Cassie was really running late, which was very unlike her. And he had nodded off in a waiting room chair, drooling, with his chin on his chest. It was a wonder that Erica, or whoever, hadn't come over to make sure he hadn't died.

Suddenly he wanted to be gone. He reached around to get his wallet – he could never remember his daughter's phone number, so she wrote it on a piece of paper and put it where the paper money went. Maybe he could get someone to call her. His fingers trembled and his fingers went past the couple of worn bills and pulled out Cassie's number. There was a second piece of paper. He took it out also and held it out as if seeing it for the first time. No name, just a number and an address, written in his grandson's hasty scrawl. A paper his grandson had given him after spending a very little time touching the screen of his phone. Something new or surprising enough to give him enough energy to stand up.

He pushed up, leaning on his cane and the arm of the chair so hard that his arms shook. Once standing upright, he stood for a second catching his breath. He looked over at Erica the receptionist, who was supposed to be watching over him. Sure enough, she was on the phone and looking down at paperwork. He glanced around the waiting room – there were no nurses or doctors in sight. The other people were involved with each other, or a magazine, or their cell phones. The little boy with hair the color of straw was now curled into the white chubby arms of his mother, sniffling quietly and sucking on a finger.

Just like Joe. Just like him.

Leaning carefully on his cane, Raymond headed towards the front door of the hospital. He thought about each step as he took it – it would not do for him to fall now and draw attention to himself now that he needed so badly to leave. He rested for a second and looked at the reflection of the room as he waited for the automatic door to open. No one was looking in his direction.

Stepping into the sunlight for the first time in a couple hours, Raymond blinked and shielded his eyes. He was standing in front of a circular driveway – a sign stating "No Parking Loading and Unloading Only" was keeping it clear of all but a grey SUV at one end. To his left the driveway ended at a long expanse of street that ran alongside the one side of the hospital. To his right the driveway ended and also ran alongside the hospital, but a few feet down was a covered bus stop. Two men were sitting in the enclosure – one was showing the other something on his cell phone. Both of them were laughing.

    Raymond carefully counted his steps as he walked down the slight incline of sidewalk next to the driveway. As he approached the bus stop he saw the two men look past him and stand – he turned to see a bus coming in his direction and he picked up the pace to get there before the bus did, though the other two men had already boarded before he got there, and the door was starting to close. He tapped on the door with his cane and the door swung open again. The inside was so dark, even with all the windows in the bus. Staring down at him from the driver's seat was a skinny man with a soft chin and tired eyes. He looked at Raymond, his jaws moving as he chewed gum. He continued to gaze sleepily at Raymond as the old man struggled to get up the three steps. Raymond paused at the top, winded from the effort, and the younger man continued to gaze at him and chew. Finally he said, "Where you going old man?"

Raymond looked up at him. Good question. YOUNG man. He looked down at his hands, which were shaking. The piece of paper was still in his hand. The bus was so quiet, as if they were all waiting for his answer. Time traveled out in front of him. When he looked up and spoke, his voice sounded as if it was coming from a great distance.

"I want to go home," he said.

CHAPTER 5

Perhaps it is that the chairs in this high school are made for the skinny asses of teenagers and not for her middle-aged spread. Or perhaps the very notion of being called in front of the principal has increased the inherent restlessness of the day and expanded it tenfold. Whatever the reason, her butt-cheeks were struggling for dominance in the seat, and so far there had been no clear-cut winner. She shifted to the left and Yay! The left cheek is in charge. Half a minute later and she shifted to the right and lo and behold the right cheek was king of the hill. Rinse and repeat – the dynamics of waiting and feeling like you're in trouble.

She looked down the hall as she shifted back to the left, moving her purse to accommodate the ever-changing geography of her lap. White walls. Blue carpet. Sterile.

Long. She could clear it in a half dozen strides or so, and the thought crossed her mind. But she doesn't know where her son was, and she was not leaving without him. All the way down the white wall was broken up with framed pieces. Student art she assumed, considering the quality. Right in front of her was a picture done with pencil and watercolor. The picture was of a young person – she couldn't tell whether it was a boy or a girl. The person's body was very small and appeared to be going off into the distance. The head, on the other hand, was very large and close to the artist and the audience. The hair was long and stood out away from the head like brown snakes. The eyes were wide and filled up the entire frame of the glasses the subject was wearing. It reminded Cassie of those sad-eyed children pictures that were popular when she was growing up – but instead of looking like they're about to brim over with tears, the eyes of this subject looked alive and happy. Not much of a nose on the subject, but below that the mouth was a big dark round O. No teeth.

  The picture next to that only held Cassie's attention for a few seconds. A bulge stood out from the canvas and was split in two and surrounded by hair. It looked so much like a vagina that she had to look away. She shifted her weight again to the right and looked away from the art down the hall that ended at a desk. The principal's secretary, a stunning black woman with hair cut very close to her head and hoop earrings, sat at the desk. She was looking down at a stack of papers in front of her, moving pages from one stack to the next. She looked up at Cassie. Her eyes said nothing.

"Mr. Bulgar will be with you in a few minutes," the secretary said. Her eyes slid to a place to the left of Cassie and rested there for a second before returning to look at her. "He has…" The secretary paused as if she wanted to say something else before settling on, "the other parents with him." And looked back down at her stack of papers.

"Other parents?" Cassie sat up. "There are 'other parents'? What does that mean? What happened?"

The secretary kept her head tilted down but lifted her eyes back up slowly. She has obviously done this for years. She smiled, a startlingly wide and expansive and open smile, probably very disarming if Cassie didn't feel so nervous. "He will be with you in a few." The smile disappeared, and she dropped her eyes back down to the task at hand. Cassie sighed and tried to look in front of her, though she had had quite enough of the happy child picture for a while. She leaned back against the wall, but her head touched the frame of another picture hanging behind her. She put her elbow on the arm of the chair and rested her cheek on her fist.

    Called before the principal. One phone call when she was halfway back to the hospital to pick up her father, and immediately she slid back forty years to when she was a senior and was caught smoking behind the dugout at the baseball field. She felt young, but not in a good way, and foolish and frightened. "There was…an incident with your son," said a smoky voice on the phone – perhaps the very secretary who was so attentive to her duties in front of her now – and Cassie swallowed hard.

    "What do you mean incident," she asked, gulping air. "I just dropped him off ten minutes ago!" There was a pause on the other end. She could almost hear the other person thinking.

    "I know. We apologize for the inconvenience. Mr. Bulgar was wondering if you could come back to school and see him for a few minutes." A statement, not a question. Cassie felt her heart pound in her chest.

"Is Joey okay?" She could hear the pitch go up in her voice. Another pause on the other end of the line before the smoky voice continued.

"Your son is not injured." Pause. "Mr. Bulgar would like to address this sooner rather than later."

"Is he in trouble?"

"Your son you mean?"

"Yes my son!" It had never occurred to her that she would be talking about the principal. Huge pause this time.

"So we'll see you back here just as soon as you can. Let them know at the front office why you're here." And Cassie's cell played three short tones to let her know the call is over. And time has turned and she is back in high school.

Resting her face on her hand, Cassie imagined for the second time today what it would feel like to be pulling tobacco smoke into her lungs. She closed her eyes and sucked air with her lips as if she was pulling on a cigarette. For the first time she heard voices through the wall. One voice in particular, a deep, gruff male voice, had gotten louder. She stopped sucking air and listened. There was the gruff voice, a calmer male voice, and a female voice that had a warbly quality to it. She strained to hear what they're saying but only caught individual words. The secretary looked up from her work and in the direction of the conversation. She glanced at Cassie before returning to her papers. Cassie looked down at stared at her cell phone, still gripped in one hand. The screen was blank – no one had called. She could no longer remember when the phone call was supposed to come – just that it would be sometime today. Instinctively she began turning the wedding ring on her finger. The voices stopped abruptly and she heard the sounds of chairs drug back across the floor. The calm voice said one last thing, there was a moment, and then a door behind her and to the left opened slowly. She was sitting against a conference room wall all that time. Around the corner came a woman in a smart business suit, jacket and skirt matching and fitting well across the chest and butt. She was made up to within an inch of her life, and had the tight facial skin of someone who has had some work done. Following her was a man, slightly shorter, solidly built and with a thick neck as if he was once a football player. He had a grey suit on and his face looked flushed. The woman hustled past Cassie on high heels, but the man paused in front of her and opened his mouth as if he was going to speak. Behind him was Principal Bulgar in white shirt, dark pants and tie loosened at the neck. Principal Bulgar had a roundness to him, round stomach, round face on shoulders without much evidence of a neck, and Cassie had often thought of Tweedle Dee or Dum when seeing him. He put his hand on the man's arm who had stopped in front of Cassie. The man looked back at the principal and closed his mouth. He hurried past Cassie to his wife, who had made it almost all the way to the end of the hall.

  Principal Bulgar stepped in front of Cassie and extended his hand. "So glad you could make it on such short notice," he said, and she recognized him as the one with the calm voice coming through the wall. She took his hand and shook it as she stood. The hand had a meaty-ness to it and the fingers were short and chubby. The hand was also slightly wet, she noticed, as if he had been sweating.

  "Something happened with my son?' She let go of his hand and stood in front of him clutching her purse and cell phone. He extended his hand past her to the door of the conference room. The secretary paused in her work and watched. Cassie walked past him and went around the corner and into the room. It was oblong and dominated by a table with three chairs on each side and one on either end. There was a laptop at the seat at the far end, so Cassie sat at the other end, as far away from the principal as possible. Bulgar, who had walked past her to head to his chair, turned and stopped to look at her.

"You don't have to sit all the way down there," he said as he continued to the seat in front of the laptop. "You can come down here. We just need to have a conversation about Joey." He spoke as if he was weighing each word for its weight and value, even more so than his secretary. That must be something they teach you when in education school. He gestured to the seat next to him, but she stays where she is and continued clutching her purse and phone with both hands and holding it in her lap. She had a fleeting thought that at least the seats in this room were made for grownups. Bulgar sat across from her and leaned back. He made a tent with his chubby fingers, putting them in front of his mouth and resting his elbows on the arms of the chair.

"As you may know, there was an incident with Joey very soon after you dropped him off at school this morning..." he spoke while looking at the screen of the laptop, as if there was a prepared script in front of him. She looked around the room before interrupting.

"Where is he?"

"Joey?" The principal seemed genuinely surprised at the question.

"Yes Joey. Can I see my son?"

As her voice escalated, the principal's slow, measured calm quality seemed to kick into overdrive. His fingers remained in tent formation in front of his face, as if the pose made him look wise.

"Joey will be with us in a few minutes. Right now he's in the clinic..."

Cassie shot out of her seat. For the first time since she entered the room her hands dropped to her sides. The hand holding her phone was wrapped tightly around the device like a fist.

"The clinic?!" What do you mean the clinic? Is my son hurt?"

Principal Bulgar stood up also. He let go of the finger tent pose and held one hand out to Cassie, as if reaching out for her.

"He's fine." Pause. "He's fine. It's just any time there's..." He paused again. "A physical altercation..."

"Physical altercation!? What the fuck does that mean??"

The curse word made the principal

blink. He dropped his hand and for the first time he looked like he didn't know what to do. He blinked again as Cassie leaned across the table towards him.

"What. Happened. To. My. Son?"

He blinked again. There was a moment where the air seemed still in the room. He lifted his arm again, gesturing to the chair where Cassie had just been sitting. She looked behind her and slowly sat down. The principal did so as well, equally slowly. For a moment the two of them looked across the table at each other. All Cassie could hear was the beating of her heart, threatening to break through her ribs. Bulgar sighed and leaned forward. He tilted the top of the laptop down so he could see her better.

"Your son got into a fight with another student."

Cassie opened her mouth to speak, though nothing came out at first. She tilted her head, closed her mouth and opened it again.

"Joey? Fight? Are you sure? He's never fought a day in his life. I'm not even sure he knows how to fight."

Bulgar smiled for the first time. "Oh but he does. He broke the other boy's nose."

Cassie sat back. Her whole body felt like Jell-O. The purse dropped to the floor as she tried to lift her arms, for what purpose she wasn't quite sure. She let them drop. And just stared at the man across the table from her. He continued, the smile playing across his face.

"It has been my experience, and I have been doing this for a long time, that when faced with confrontation, people have two choices. Either fight. Or flight. Unfortunately for Joey, he chose fight."

Someone knocked on the door behind her, a sudden noise that caused her to jump. "Come in," Bulgar called, and Cassie turned to see the door open and the stunning secretary with hoop earrings peered through.

"Mr. Bulgar. He's here."

Bulgar waved in the direction of the door. "Send him in."

The hooped earrings withdrew and the door swung open wide. Joey stepped in, his head hung so low that the only part of his face she could see was his nose and chin. His skin was wet. His head was a mass of wavy brown hair, a DNA gift from his dad.

"Have a seat." Bulgar gestured to the chairs to Cassie's left. For the first time Joey looked up. The wet on his face was from tears. He looked at his mother then at the chairs. He sank into the middle one, sliding as far down as he could, his wet chin buried into his chest, his hands hidden under the desk. He looked brittle. Her beautiful baby boy, the child she had because a guy named Dwight who wore cowboy boots asked her to the prom thirty-five years ago.

Principal Bulgar was doing the tent thing with his fingers again. He directed his attention at Joey, who looked at neither adult.

"You know why your mother is here, right?" He asked the teenager. Joey nodded while staring down into his lap. Bulgar turned to Cassie. His tone was firm and even as he spoke. "This morning your son assaulted another student in the courtyard."

"He was calling me names!" Joey's head jerked up as he spoke, his wavy hair flying away from his face. She saw his eyes for the first time. They were pleading with her. "Mom, he..." His voice faded, and he looked down at the table. His fingers on one hand were picking frantically at the nails on the other hand.

"Yes." Principal Bulgar paused before speaking, to no one in particular. "He said the other boy..."

Cassie held her hand up, the palm out to the principal. He stopped in mid-sentence. With her arm still up, she turned to her son. "Wait. What?" She looked back and forth between the man and the boy, waiting for one of them to answer. The adult looked stunned, so she asked the boy again.

"What. Did. He. Do?"

The voice was muffled but the answer was clear. "He called me names."

Cassie whipped back to Bulgar so quickly her vision went blurry for a second. Her arm went down slowly as she glared across the table.

"So let me get this straight. My son is bullied..." She hit the word as hard as she could. "And HE'S the one in the principal's office?" Both hands were on top of the table in front of her, the fingers spread wide. Principal Bulgar was looking down at his hands clasped together in his lap. It looked like he was praying. He looked back up and met her gaze. The edges of his mouth twitched as if he couldn't keep them from lifting.

"That's because the other boy is at the hospital. Remember he..." Bulgar pointed in Joey's direction, "broke the other boy's nose. Yes, bullying is bad. But so is assault. If your son had walked away and reported the incident it would have been one thing. But he didn't. He swung. And now a child is injured."

Cassie listened to herself breathe. She

continued looking at the principal, though her eyes glazed over so that she didn't see him. "Some child," she said under her breath.

Bulgar didn't even blink as he continued. "The district is very clear about this. Three days suspension and anger management classes..."

"Classes?!" Cassie's eyes snapped back into focus. "Who in the fuck is going to pay for that?" Joey lifted his head to look at his mother, his mouth open. The principal's eyes widened and his cheeks flushed. He was still red when he answered.

"I can give you a list of places approved by the county that offer classes. The prices are very affordable..."

"I'll bet..." It was out before she knew it. The principal's eyes, returning to normal, widened again. Nonetheless he soldiered on.

"The point is, that is his only option. Suspension and classes. He needs to learn that choices have consequences. Perhaps he can be taught to make better choices..."

At that moment something dark and awful, lying dormant like a seed in dirt, began to bloom inside Cassie. As the blossoms unfurled and opened, they pushed themselves jagged and sharp and hard through her ribs and out through her skin.

They cut through the air and filled up the room so that she could no longer see. They sliced and curled themselves backward into yesterday and then the day before that and the day before that, blocking out the sun in every direction as far back as she could remember. Surrounded and crushed and blind, she felt something rise up in her throat. She turned her head one direction and another. Her son was out there somewhere in all of this. She had to save him from this terrible thing that threatened to kill her.

She was on her feet so fast that her chair tipped over. The dark awful thing around her fluttered away from her body and came back and settled around her. Pushing back against a pressure wrapped all around her body and cutting into skin, she lifted her arm in the direction of her son. Her lungs couldn't expand, so her voice when she spoke sounded pinched and tight.

"Fine. We'll do the classes. And I guess my son and I will have a nice little vacation together." She turned in the direction of her extended hand. Joey was there. She could see again.

At least she could see him.

"Come on Joey. Let's go pick up your grandpa."

CHAPTER 6

    The bus had only a handful of riders. The two men sitting close, a man in a tie reading a newspaper, a large woman cradling two plastic bags of groceries in her lap, a young woman with white wires coming out of her ears and gazing out the window. Raymond could sit anywhere. A sign above the seats facing each other at the front of the bus says PLEASE SAVE FOR ELDERLY WOMEN WITH INFANTS. Because there is not a comma between ELDERLY and WOMEN, the sign gives Raymond pause. Considering that he won't encounter any elderly women with infants on this particular ride, he turned to sit. He saw the rest of the bus as he did so. Everyone else is seated facing his way. He hesitated and looked at the driver. He can only see the back of his head, hair cut short like he was in the army, skin red on his neck. But Raymond can see the man's eyes reflected in the rearview mirror and they are watching him. He is waiting for the old man. Raymond turned away from the driver and headed slowly down the aisle towards the back of the bus. He felt flushed, as if he was exerting himself too hard. He heard the bus idling. When he walked past the two men he heard them whispering to one another. Their heads were bent towards each other and one has his arm around the shoulders of the other. Music came off the young woman with the white wires, slow quiet notes from a guitar playing under a voice mumbling words he couldn't understand. The rows behind her on both sides of the aisle were empty. These were the next to the last rows on the bus. He sat catty-corner from the young woman with the music, his butt in the seat first before swinging his legs in. He looked up to the front at the driver, whose eyes drop from view in the mirror. The bus roared to life and lurched forward.

    Raymond looked out the window. Once the bus moved past the buildings belonging to the hospital, nothing looked familiar. Unlike the rural area where he used to live, which was long unbroken stretches of countryside, this was all buildings. The storefronts sold all manner of merchandise he had absolutely no need for – cellular phones, tires, tattoos, medical supplies, Jesus. Okay, well maybe he still had need for one of those. Medical supplies. The buildings would go by the window slowly at first, then so fast as the bus sped up that he couldn't read the signs. He focused on one image but it would blur past before he could even see it. Or he would see it like a memory seconds after he looked at it. He felt dizzy. Finally, he turned away from the window and looked at the back of the heads of the other passengers. Like him they didn't seem to be going anywhere fast.

  He heard a ding over the sound of the engine and the bus slowed down. It lurched again when it came to a stop so that Raymond held onto the seat in front of him. He heard the girl's music again, which was drowned out by the bus. The woman with the bags of groceries got off – three people, a young couple holding hands and a nun carrying a Bible, got on. The bus was starting to fill up. The nun sat in one of the reserved seats, but the young couple, not much older than his grandson, walked past him and sat in the long seat across the back of the bus. Raymond does not turn to look at them but heard them scoot across the seat towards each other once they sat down.

In fifteen minutes the bus was almost full. The male couple was gone. So was the businessman with the tie and the newspaper. The girl with the music in her ears was still on, her eyes closed and her hands nodding to some kind of rhythm. The nun was still in the reserved seats, fingering a rosary and moving her lips. She was sandwiched in between people who were not elderly or women or elderly women with babies. The young couple is still behind him doing god knows what. The boy whispered something and the girl giggled, high pitched squealing that prompted people all the way in the front (but not the driver) to look over their shoulders to the back.

Raymond had rows and rows of backs of heads to study. Some of the shoulders were dotted with water since it had started to rain outside. Nobody had seated themselves next to him. He didn't scoot all the way over to the window when he first sat down and was now sitting in the middle of the seat. He thought that to the casual observer it may seem as if he was occupying more than his fair share of space. He smiled at the thought. A house reduced down to a room in a house, with all of his belongings in a box, seemed more to him like shrinking.

No one made eye contact, even when they turned around to look at the young couple. Maybe they're afraid old age was contagious. It occurred to him that maybe he should have asked someone where the bus was going. The street names meant nothing to him. But he could tell which direction he was heading. From many years of driving a tractor down rows of corn and soy beans pushing their way through clods of dirt, he could tell from the sun which direction was north. And this was north. North was good. North was where home was.

  The brakes shrieked as the bus stopped suddenly. The driver reached over and pulled a handle and the doors sighed as they opened. At first Raymond saw no one come up the steps into the bus, though he heard grunts and groans and objects hitting steps. Finally pink hair appeared above the panel blocking the steps from the seats. The pink hair bobbed down out of sight and after a second a hand came out from behind the panel and tossed a backpack onto floor next to the driver. The hands disappeared again and re-appeared, tossing what looked like a diaper bag next to the backpack. A third toss and a shoulder bag landed on top of the other two. A hand, nails polished deep purple, gripped the top of the panel and the owner of the pink hair hauled herself into view with a baby on her hip.

    The young woman smiled broadly at the bus driver, the edges of her bright red mouth almost disappearing into cheeks so round and chubby they looked like they had food in them. A tiny piece of metal like the edge of a horseshoe dangled from each nostril. Her hair was plastered to one side and hung over the right side in pick points. The left side of her head was a crew cut like he wore in the sixties. Her left ear had a row of rings pierced in it from top to bottom. Her round eyes were lined in black. Bracelets and chains adorned her wrists and neck. A dark green coat drug across the floor as she stepped to her bags.

    The fat baby with legs like sausages wrapped around her waist could be his mother's son. Same chubby cheeks and round eyes. Same pale complexion. A blue blanket (Raymond's wife would have had an exact name for that shade of blue, being the stickler for color specifics that she was) was loosely wrapped around his body, though his fingers were wriggling free and waving in the direction of his mother's ample breasts. One hand solidly gripped a plastic giraffe which he held to his mouth. As she bent over to dig through her backpack he tilted his head to the ceiling of the bus then stretched around to look at the passengers. And then he smiled and Raymond remembered how much he loved babies.

    The change jingled as she paid the fare. She bent over and zipped up the backpack before she piled the bags back onto herself like she was her own pack mule. The driver watched her, expressionless, only leaning back when she threw the diaper bag over her shoulder and almost hit him in the nose. The other riders watched this struggle between human and belongings silently as well, some leaning into the aisle to get a better view. It almost seemed to Raymond that the whole bus was holding its breath to see how the conflict would play itself out. Finally all three bags were defying gravity and sticking out at various angles away from her body and she began her journey down the aisle. People who had leaned out to watch sat back up and suddenly became very interested in the view out the window. The young woman mumbled "Pardon me" and "Excuse me" as she made her way to the back of the bus. No one looked at her or got up to offer her their seat. The baby, however, leaned as far away from his mother as he could, reaching towards people's face and hair with his pudgy fingers, cooing and swinging the plastic giraffe towards people's heads.

Finally she stood in front of Raymond's seat, her face red from the effort. She looked him squarely in the eye. "Well Mister, it looks like it's you and me," she said huffing slightly. Raymond looked around him, even though it was obvious she was talking to him.

"Uh...okay..." He looked down at the seat, realized there wasn't enough room for her, her three bags and her child. He scooted over as close to the window as he could get and she was down in one large movement, the seat releasing air like a tire as she sat. There was so much movement as she settled in that he couldn't take her eyes off her. Half of her things were still in the aisle and the baby was at a weird angle away from her body as if he wanted to get down and walk. Raymond opened his mouth and closed it once twice three times before any more sound came out.

"Is there...I don't know, anything I can..."

She didn't even let him finish. "Sure. Here take this for a minute would you? Raymond held his arms out. And suddenly he was looking the baby boy face to face. The child's eyes were opened wide as if he had been startled, but then he waved his tiny arms and stuck the giraffe in his mouth, getting the plastic shiny with drool as he sucked on it. Raymond looked over at the mother, holding the child away from his body but she was bent over going through one of the bags. She looked up and met Raymond's gaze. She shrugged.

"He's a great kid. I promise." And yeah, I know, I shouldn't be handing him off to just anyone. But it's not like you're gonna run away with him, right? I'm blocking your way. And I'm just betting you couldn't get very far without me catching up to you." She paused and continued to search through a bag. "Right?" She waited for an answer. Raymond nodded. "It's alright," she said, almost more into the diaper bag than to him, "You can hold him closer. He's teething, but I don't think he'll bite. And he's clean. I changed his poopy diaper before we got on the bus." And with that she began moving items from one bag to the other.

Raymond looked at the baby. The child's whole chin was wet at this point, and a drop of drool was dangling off the giraffe's foot. The baby's brown eyes searched Raymond's face, and as the old man pulled him in closer, he reached up to touch Raymond on the nose. She was right. He smelled like powder and baby shampoo. He was looking at Raymond so intently. The old man wondered if this would be something the child would remember when he was older. Raymond's oldest memory was of his mother's face. He had no idea how old he was. He was looking up, and her head was backlit by the sun. She was frowning though Raymond had no memory of why. From that point on, however, every time he thought of his mother, stern and unbending and mostly lacking in the warmth he would experience in later mothers, that was the image that came to mind first. Raymond didn't want this little boy, if he were to remember this moment, to think of a frown. Raymond smiled, stretching his cheeks so far they almost hurt. The baby squealed, threw his head back and kicked the blue blanket away from his little legs.

"Mary's the name by the way." Mary wiped her hand on her coat before offering it to Raymond. Bracelets clanked as they shook hands.

"Raymond."

"Raymond. Nice solid name. Goes with your nice solid face. Kind face." She pointed at the baby who Raymond was now cradling. The child was reaching up and touching the edge of the old man's chin. "And that there's

Adam. As in Adam the first man." Mary chuckled. "Might be the last, if I have anything to say about it. Of course, there wasn't really no plans for a first one. But here he is. That's a long story right there in and of itself." She put the backpack on her lap and began shoving the other two bags under the seat in front of her. "Was gonna name him Jesus, on account of his momma and poppa were named Mary and Joseph."

  She stopped and looked for a reaction from Raymond. He looked down and pursed his lips at Adam, bouncing him up and down gently in his arms. She pointed at the two of them. "He likes you. That's good. He takes to people, which I think is good. And he likes the bouncing, though he just ate about a half hour ago, so continue at your own risk." She laughed at Raymond when he jerked his head to look at her. "Just kiddin.' You should be fine." She sits back and sighs. "Yeah, I kid you not. Mary and Joseph. Could we have been any more of a religious cliché if we tried?" She shrugged. "Well, maybe if we'd named the kid Jesus we woulda been. But Joseph thought he would get made fun of. So we went with Adam instead. And that. As it turns out," she sighed heavily as she said this. "That was the last thing Joe contributed to Adam's upbringing."

"Ah..." Adam was sitting up and on Raymond's knee. Raymond was moving his leg up and down and each bounce sent the child into peals of laughter. He reached over and touched Raymond, reaching into the pockets on his sweater. "It sounds like there's a story there."

"Honey. I could write a book." She fingered the rings in her ear with one hand. "But you know, it's a tale as old as time." She looked sideways at Raymond. "You like that Disney reference?"

Raymond stopped bouncing his knee and looked over at Mary. She shook her head and continued. "You know..." she started singing. "Tale as old as time..." Adam looked over at his mother and clapped his hands. The giraffe was gone. Raymond looked around him to see if it was dropped.

"You know. Beauty and the..." She waits for a response but he says nothing but bounced the baby again.

"Never mind. It's cool." She laughed and went back to her story. "But it is that classic story. I'm working in a bar. Not working a bar, if you know what I mean..."

"Sure," Raymond said, even though he's not at all sure he does.

"...but working in a bar as a bartender.

Joseph was lead singer in a ska band..."

"What's ska?" Raymond asked. Adam was pushing at the old man's cheek with his two chubby hands.

"Ska? It's like reggae, but not..."

"What's reggae?" This time Raymond's question is muffled since Adam's hands are pulling at his lower lip.

"What's reggae?"

"Yes reggae. Is it like Perry Como?"

Mary laughed. "Yes. It's like Perry Como. Very, very close. So anyway Joseph's singing ska...I mean Perry Como...in my bar and he says all the right things and voila..." She holds out her hands to her stuff and her son. "Here we are." She reached out to Adam, who immediately grabbed her finger. "Fast forward six months and suddenly, out of the blue, he has a tour. They're dinky little bars in towns I've never heard of. But it's a gig. And he's gone."

She stopped and Raymond looked over at her. Adam's hands are all over his face. Mary's face was resting in her hands.

"So that's why we're here today. He's in Virginia. Some place called Stafford. He's Adam's father." She stopped for a second before she continued. "And I have to know. I have to know if he's going to be one."

Raymond didn't know what to say. He

looked from Mary back to Adam. The little boy was looking at him intently, his mouth hanging open, his lips moving like he's trying to form words. The old man turned back to Mary.

"Mary I..." he began.

Just then Adam's little head jerked forward, and suddenly the side of Raymond's face was wet. He turned back to Adam whose mouth was covered in applesauce. The boy smiled broadly at the old man and clapped his hand before sticking one in his mouth to suck off undigested pieces of apple. Raymond put his hand slowly up to the left side of his face. More chunks of apple and sauce. He turned slowly to Mary, vomited applesauce in one hand, vomit-covered cooing baby in the other. Her eyes are so wide he can almost see himself in them.

"I guess the bouncing wasn't such a good idea after all. Applesauce is usually his favorite. I am so, so, soooo sorry." And then she sprang into action, diving into the diaper bag, unzipping it in one swift motion and burying a hand deep into the contents. A few seconds of rummaging produced a container of handi-wipes. She held out her arms to Adam, who does the same and fell forward into his mother's body.

Raymond sat quietly watching Mary

clean up her son. She wiped his face in short quick strokes, holding his chin as she goes. The boy moved his head in a circle trying to pull away, but he's laughing like he's playing a game. This whole routine reminded Raymond of his daughter and grandson. Cassie waited so long to have a child that by the time she was 36 and holding Joey in her arms, she didn't quite know what to do with him. She treated him like an object, something to clean and feed but nothing to attach too much affection to for fear he would break under the weight of it. But then a touch that was meant to be all business would turn into a caress, and suddenly she was confused and angry. That stood in direct contrast to his wife who lost one baby so she clung to the other two, as if the first one had wandered off instead of dying in childbirth. She squeezed so tightly that both of them popped out and away. And one of them, the one with the same name as Adam's daddy, never came back. He looked at Mary, who stuck her thumb in her mouth and wiped a stubborn speck of vomit off Adam's cheek. She held the container of wipes out to Raymond. "You want one?"

    He wiped the side of his face and shook his head. He looks up to the front of the bus. "My stop's coming up anyways."

"You good then? I mean, you need to get somewhere I can help you with? Adam and I are on our way to the Greyhound bus station to..." She laughed for a second. "I know, taking the bus to the bus. That's my life, right?" She tilted her head as she looked at Raymond. Her son reached up to the rings in her ear and she swatted him away with one hand. "Anyway, I used to be a girl scout. You'd never guess it to look at me now, but I was. And I feel like I should help you with somethin'..."

"Nah. You've been good."

"Not even cross the street? I could do that."

"Nah..." he reached up and rang the bell to stop the bus. "You're awfully sweet though." He looked down into his lap where he saw drops of undigested apple. He took a deep breath before he continued. "You've got a plan. You need to go forward with this little one here and move on ahead with that plan. Plus..." he looked out the window as the bus slowed down. "I don't know exactly where I'm going. So you shouldn't be going there with me."

Mary held Adam to her chest. The little boy peeked out from the coat at Raymond.

"I thought you said this was..."

"I know what I said. My stop is comin'

up." He paused. "As I said, you're awfully sweet. I thank you for that."

And Adam, as if to add to the conversation, held out his arms to Raymond to be held.

Raymond looked at him for a long moment then up at his mother. She met his gaze and in the silence that followed the brakes shrieked as the bus came to a stop. Without a word, Mary swung her legs out into the aisle so that Raymond could get by. The journey to the front of the bus seemed twice as long as the trip to the back did. This time people looked up as he shuffled past. No doubt he smelled like apple. Or vomit. Or both. He turned at the steps and saw Adam standing up in his mother's lap. Her body was curved around his and she was whispering in his ear. She had hold of his wrist and moved his arm up and down. The little boy opened and closed his fingers. Raymond waved back. Once he got down the steps he paused and watched the bus as it roared past him on its way up the street.

Drops of rain kissed him on the face. He reached up to rub them away and his arm brushed against something solid in the pocket of his sweater. He reached in and pulled out Adam's plastic giraffe. White with brown dots, the giraffe gazed up at him with black dots for eyes. Raymond looked back at him for a second, shaking his head and smiling. Then he put the giraffe back in his pocket and looked up at the sky for a second before turning towards the north and trudging slowly up the sidewalk, leaning heavily on his cane.

CHAPTER 7

The inside of the car was excruciatingly quiet. It was only fourteen miles between the school and the hospital, but Cassie was feeling like the mother whose little girl was sucked into the TV set by evil spirits in an early 1980s horror movie she saw on a date once. In one scene the mother hears her child scream at the end of the hall upstairs and as she starts to run the director did this really cool thing where he stretched out the hall and made it much longer, like she could never make it that far to save her child. At least at the time Cassie thought it was cool. Now thirty years later it was her life. The fourteen miles might as well have been the distance between Florida and California – which was about how far away she felt from her child right now.

Joey must have felt it too because his

body was plastered about as far against the passenger door as he could make it. Both of his legs were turned away from her and his hair, that beautiful blonde hair he got from his father, fell across his face. His nose was pressed to the glass but his eyes were looking down. He looked as if he were sleeping – he had folded himself into a similar position when he was a little boy and curled into the crook of her as he grew drowsy from listening to her read a bedtime story. But she knew he was not asleep now. He sniffled and lifted the arm that wasn't smashed against the side of the car to wipe his nose.

    She wanted to reach over and touch him, put her hand on his arm and feel the heat rising off of him. But he would only pull away from her like she was poison, pushing himself hard into the car door as if he could go through it and out into the air. And she couldn't stand that. A look over in his direction might make him flinch. So she glanced instead in the direction of the rearview mirror on his side, using the feigned casualness she and her friends would use when scoping out boys in the cafeteria in high school. With her peripheral vision she studied him, daring herself to turn her whole head in his direction. She lost the dare. Instead she looked ahead of her at the traffic on the road. The day had turned grey but couldn't commit to a full rainstorm. Fat drops of water came apart when they touched her windshield. A few drops here. Pause. A few more drops there. A single swipe of the wipers took care of things. And the process started all over again. Drops pause drops swipe. There was a rhythm to it. Like counting off moments until the next time. Like breathing. She looked down at her hands gripping the wheel. The knuckles were white.

"So..." she floated the word out into the air easily, hoping for a soft landing. She also hoped for a whole sentence to follow it, but what came out is only one word. "Names."

"What?" The word came out long and drawn out from underneath Joey's hair. It sounded drowsy. He did not move.

"Names." She paused then jumped in. "You said he called you names."

"Yeah." Again with the muffled sound. "So?"

"Well you didn't say. What kinds of names did he call you?"

"Really?" His head finally turned towards her. He reached up with his free hand and pushed the hair away from his face. His fingers were delicate and gentle as he stroked strands away from his mouth. "Mom, really?" This time he was the one to pause as he looked at her. She almost smiled as she thought to herself, gee, I wonder where he got that from? as he continued, his voice starting to take on an edge.

"What does it matter? I'm the one who got in trouble." He turned his head away from her to look out the window.

"You got me there." She kept her face forward, watching drops splat against her windshield. "You are in so much goddamn trouble…"

"Mom!" Joey shook his head and looked sideways at his mother. "I am so gonna get you a swear jar."

"What the fuck is a swear jar?" This time it was Cassie's turn to shake her head. Joey's body jerked forward and he snorted and covered his mouth and suddenly the air inside the car was lighter. She could breathe again without choking.

"Listen, I don't know the Heimlich, so you're gonna be on your own here." She dared to take her eyes fully off the road for the first time. His body moved back and forth in the seat, his forehead almost touching the glove compartment. He lifted his face. It was flushed. He looked at Cassie and he was smiling.

"Mom, Mom, Mom..." He tossed his gorgeous hair back and forth slowly. "Do you kiss your mother with that mouth?"

"No. But I kiss you..."

"Ewww..." His whole body pulled away from her side of the car and he made a gagging sound. "No you don't!"

"I don't?" She reached over and rubbed her hand on the top of his head. He didn't flinch or pull away. For a second she imagined he bent his head into her hand. But only for a moment. Then the traffic stopped in front of her and she looked back through the windshield dotted with raindrops. She hadn't turned on the wipers for a while. Her hand lingered, briefly entangled in his hair. She wrapped her fingers around his skull, staying with the embrace for a second before pulling away to grip the wheel.

"You got me there..." She sighed deeply. "Truer words..." Her voice trailed off. As the traffic started back up again she looked back at her son. He was combing his long hair back away from his face gently with his fingers. He was so delicate when he did that. It seemed new, the delicate thing with the hands and the hair. Or maybe it had always been there, but she just hadn't been watching. Somewhere a horn honked and she focused back on the traffic as she spoke.

"So…" She drew the first word out, thinking how to phrase the rest. "Speaking of words. And things like that…"

"Mom!" The smile flamed out, but at least he didn't turn away from her. He sighed and dropped his head and she felt it begin, this walk they were about to take, not hand in hand but at least side by side, down this road they'd never traveled before. She swallowed and continued.

"So. The names." She waited and listened to her son sigh again. "What exactly did this kid call you?"

She waited. "Well…" he began. It sounded as if he were weighing his words very carefully. "I might have lied about that. Just a little…"

"Joseph!!"

"No no no! His hands flew up and waved in the air like he was erasing the previous statement. "I don't mean…I don't mean lie exactly. I mean, he did call me a name…"

"But…"

"But what?"

Joey hesitated for a second. "It wasn't what he said so much that made me… made me..."

"Beat the living crap out of him?"
"Well I wouldn't put it like..."
"Joey."
"Yeah okay sure."

Cassie stared ahead while she was driving, but her mind was on the road that she and her son had started down together. There were a lot of little side paths and she was trying as hard as she could not to stray down one of these paths or give up and turn back.

"So okay..." She thought for a second before continuing. "What exactly did he say to you. Let's get back to that."

"Uh..." Joey glanced sideways at his mother again. He began to pick at his nails.

"Are we gonna need the swear jar for this?"

"Oh yeah." He nodded his head vigorously. The nail picking became more intense.

"Okay. And?" She turned on the wipers and watched them smear water across her field of vision. No answer from the passenger side of the car. She glanced over. Joey was rubbing one hand over his forehead.

"Oh Jesus Christ Joey, just tell me what the other kid said!"

A chuckle escaped from Joey's mouth

but ended abruptly as if it hurt his throat.

"He uh...He said...He called me a motherfucking cocksucking faggot."

Cassie was never so glad to come to a stop light so she could brake the car. She continued to look at her son, who was beginning to fold in on himself again. She opened her mouth but no sound came out. The light turned green and she turned back to her driving. As she moved through the intersection she turned on the windshield wipers and left them on. Once twice three times they swiped the glass. They went back and forth in front of her eyes nine times before she spoke again.

"Well then...Correct me if I'm wrong, but I think those first two words contradict each other. Am I right?"

He was sniffing, but a sound gurgled up through it that might have meant he enjoyed what she said. "Yeah," he said, "You're right about that." He wiped his hand across his nose.

"So...Let's get rid of that first word for a second." She reached up and pretended to yank the word out of mid-air. She rolled down the window and mimed throwing the word out. Joey looked up and watched her intently.

"Okay, so take that word away. What

we've got left...is it true?" The words were out before she even knew she was thinking them. It was like it had always been there waiting to be spoken. And now it was out there, in the air, floating between them. She heard Joey's car seat make sounds as he shifted – whether away or towards her she couldn't tell. She listened to his ragged breathing and turned off the wipers. The rain was picking up, and she really needed them, but the sound was more than she could take. She leaned forward, looking so hard through the wet glass that her eyes hurt. Finally she turned the wipers back on. Off in the distance there was actually blue sky. Weird weather. And that is when she saw it.

Stripes of color arcing toward the horizon. A motherfucking rainbow.

"I can't. Frigging. Believe it." She leaned farther towards the glass. She heard Joey start to speak but then stop, and when she glanced to the side she could see him leaning forward as well and looking out the window with her. For a long time there was no sound except the wipers going back and forth, the heartbeat of the car as it moved towards the color.

"So I'm having a rough day, and I'm all good and ready to wallow in my misery, and the world won't even let me do that. It's like that friend who won't leave you alone. Always tapping you on the shoulder and saying, 'Look, everything's not so bad. Look how pretty and gorgeous things really are.'" She felt her throat catch as she spoke.

"Yeah," Joey agreed, his nose practically touching the glass. "Mother nature can sure be a bitch sometimes. Can't she Mom?"

They turned to each other at that and burst into laughter. He was smiling and that was her rainbow. Which kept the smile on her face as well, long after the laughter died down. She reached over and put his head in her Vulcan death grip again. This time she was sure he tilted into it – just for a second, certainly short enough to deny it later if he had to. But she knew it was there. She let go and brought her hand back to the wheel.

"You know that hurts don't you Mom?" At least he was acknowledging the contact.

"Oh stop being a wussy." She was still smiling. The air inside the car was breathable once more, full of oxygen.

"That is your son. A big old fat wussy."

She felt a beat, a slight hitch before she continued. "What else is my son?"

She looked out the window when she asked but she could feel her son's eyes on her. Another beat. The wipers did their thing.

"So we're going to have this conversation now?" He paused as if he actually thought she was going to answer. "Well okay then." Another beat. "One thing your son is not. And that is a motherfucking cock sucking faggot."

"He's not?" Another beat.

"Nah. We already talked about the first word. And that last one..." She looked over at him then. He was looking at her without blinking. He continued. "Faggot is so last century. If anything I'm gender fluid."

"Gender fluid? What the hell does that mean? You like both boys and girls?"

"No, that's bisexual. Gender fluidity is...well, it's hard to explain. I'll look it up on Urban Dictionary someday. Maybe you'll understand it then."

"Maybe. So..." She really needed to take one of the side paths now so she searched for the right words to continue. "So if he had called you gender fluid you wouldn't have beat the crap out of him?"

"Mom. No." He sighed as if he was in the presence of a small simple child and he was tired of explaining things to her. "I told you. It wasn't the words."

"So if it wasn't the words, what was it?"

"Uh..." He took a deep breath. "It was

the boy."

"Aaaahhhh…" She drew it out like it was more than one syllable. A light was coming on in her head. "So you have something else to tell me?" She needed to watch the traffic, but she really needed to see her son at this moment. He bobbed his head up and down. She reached over and put her hand on her son's knee. "Okay then. Tell me about the boy."

And he did. He told her about Jason – "Your grandfather would say that was a good name," she told Joey – the boy in his Biology class with a smile like looking at honey through a jar. With deep creases in his cheeks ("Those are called dimples," she said to her son. "Whatever Mom," he sighed, exasperated.) every time that smile appeared. The barely grunted acknowledgements they exchanged every time they passed each other in the hall. The looks up from the textbook, held a couple seconds too long, during study time in class. "All the stereotypical bullshit you would expect," Joey said. "Swear Jar," his mom said and he laughed. And then there was the day Joey closed his locker and Jason was there, standing and looking at him like he had seen him for the first time. The exchange of words that followed could have been construed as both a conversation and asking someone out on a date.

"Hey."

"Hey."

"How you doing?"

"Okay. You?"

"Good."

Awkward pause.

"Kirsten's having a party this Saturday."

"I heard."

"You gonna go?"

"Thought about. You?"

"Thought about it."

"K. Maybe I'll see you there."

"K."

And so Joey went ("Oh, so that's what you did on Saturday," Cassie said. "I told you I was going there," Joey said. "You said you were going to hang out. You didn't say there would be a bunch of people there." "Mom, do you wanna hear about this or not?"). And it was at Kirsten's house that Joey opened a door, thinking it was a bathroom but discovering Jason going through the drawers of Kirsten's parents in the master bedroom. The next part of the story was mercifully short of details ("Thanks for that," Cassie said, "I don't need that much information."), though the upshot was that Joey thought the other boy liked him. Really liked him. So imagine Joey's surprise when the following Monday when he ran into Jason in the courtyard. In the presence of other boys Jason didn't flash his smile like honey. And the names. And the blood, which Joey, on top of the other boy, saw on his own shirt before he saw it on Jason's face. Hands balled into fists swinging through the air in a blur. Being pulled off by an adult.

    Cassie nodded her head through it all. Now she understood. Or was beginning to. She and her son had taken this trip and managed to stay on the path and come at the end. Still side by side. They could work on hand in hand later. Joey was no longer upset and that was a very good thing. Maybe she could even help or offer one or two words of advice. God knows she had enough experience that she might have one or two nuggets of wisdom to offer. That would certainly be one good thing that would come from all of it.

    But that would have to wait. They were turning into the parking lot of hospital. Time to pick up her father and whatever he was bringing with him on this latest trip to the doctor. She looked up into the sky as she parked the car. The sky was clearing and there was no longer any rain. She scanned for the ribbons of color but could no longer see them.

And she really, really needed to check her phone.

CHAPTER 8

In the forty-nine years Raymond was a farmer he got into the habit of studying the clouds. His children tried to tell him the names of them when they were in school, but he could never remember. He just knew size and shape and color and what that all meant. White little wisps of things streaking across the sky meant he had the day, either so hot the inside of his mouth dried up or so cold his nose stung, to get a good chunk of work done. Even mountains of clouds, flat on the bottom and piled high on top, still meant the day was his. A long bank of grey clouds, stretching across the horizon and inching towards him meant something was coming – either cold or rain – and he needed to hurry. Dark clouds, of course, meant rain was here. Rain was what he wanted. A good fifteen minute downpour to soak the ground and water the corn and soybeans and he was a happy man.

But too hard and too much and it would wash the seed away. Or too little and it was just irritating. It was like someone was spitting on your face every few seconds. And today he was irritated. It was bad enough that the one leg was weak and he had to use a cane, or that he had a pushing on his chest when he tried to breathe, which was a constant reminder of the doctor's visit from a little while ago and the news that came with it. Now he had to deal with a drop of water on his cheeks and then another one and then another. It no longer felt like someone kissing his skin – because it was cold it almost felt like needles in his skin. But home. I want to go home, he thought. Home. It became a chant he said to himself, breathing air into lungs that hurt and saying the words as he breathed out. Home.

He came to a corner and stopped, leaning on the cane with both hands. He looked up at the street signs, though none of the names meant anything to him. He stepped off the curb with one foot and then flinched and swayed as a blue SUV honked at him as it drove past. He heard the muffled shouting of the driver. He understood the tone though not any of the words. He looked up at the street light and saw he had a Do Not Walk sign. He lifted his leg back onto the curb and waited. He took off his glasses speckled with water and felt around on his sweater for a dry area to wipe them on. He put them back on but he had only managed to streak the water across the glass. He took them off again and wiped his face with his hand, trying to rub the feeling of the needles away.

"Mister, do you need some help?"

The sound of the voice coming from behind him on the sidewalk made him jump. He leaned into the cane for a moment, waiting for his heart to slow down and see who was talking to him. It always took a moment to plan for big events. Like turning around. The voice persisted.

"I said. Do you need some help? Sir?"

He pivoted slowly to see the source of the voice. A little girl, maybe twelve, stood there looking up at him. Her eyes were large and shaped like almonds, white against her brown skin. Her black hair hung down to her shoulders in massive amounts of tight curls which glistened with drops of water. Nestled, almost buried, on the top of her head was a dark green beret which topped off the dark green (once again, Joanne would have had a very distinct name for exactly what kind of green it was) dress. Across all of it was the green sash of the girl scout uniform. In her arms she cradled a large shopping bag. Out of the top sprouted oblong boxes of every color -blue and orange and yellow and red and purple. Raymond smiled at her and she tilted her head and tried again.

"So you okay?"

Raymond chuckled. "Well that is the question isn't it?" He shifted his weight on his cane and started to turn away.

"Because if you aren't, I can help you."

He stopped and looked back at the girl. "You can help me?"

"Sure." She shifted the shopping bag to one hip and used the free hand to gesture at herself. "That..." She paused as she executed an elaborate flourish with her hand down the length of her uniform. "That is what we do. There are all kinds of things I can do for you. If you're choking, I can perform the Heimlich on you. Or at least..." She paused again and looked him up and down, no doubt comparing his height to hers. "At least I could try. If you're unconscious and you've stopped breathing, I could give you mouth to mouth. If you've fallen and you can't get up I can help you up. And if you have trouble walking, I can –" She gestured to the sidewalk in front of them – "help you across the street. As a matter of fact, that's one of our specialties." She took a step towards him and pointed at her sash, which was adorned with all number of brightly-colored knickknacks. "They train us. Then we do it. Then they give us badges for it."

Raymond chuckled again. "They give you a badge for helping old people across the street."

"Sure." She shrugged before bringing the bag of cookies back in front of her and wrapping both her arms around it. "Public service things. Like I said, there are all kinds of things we can do. All kinds of badges." She heaved the bag higher and hugged it closer. "I'm real good at building a fire." She shrugged. "Like I'm ever going to use that around here." She looked down into the bag overflowing with brightly-colored boxes. "What I'm bad at selling things. At selling I truly suck." A silence settled between them. Raymond looked at the ground.

"Aren't you supposed to be in school?" he asked finally.

"Yeah..." she said, drawing out the one word like it was at least three syllables. Now it was her turn to look down, staring down into the bag and past the cookie boxes like she could see through to the bottom.

"So...?" Raymond had looked up and

gazed at her down-turned lashes. They flickered but didn't look back.

"So," she shrugged, holding out the shopping bag. "There's this. All of this. Every. Single. Box they gave me at the beginning of the sale. Which was – what? – two weeks ago. I don't have grandparents in the area who'll snatch up every box you have because they love to see you smile when you hand you the cookies and they hand you the cash. And my parents. Well...my parents..." Her eyes grazed past his and squinted up at the sky. She shifted the cookies to her hip again and held her free palm up in the air. She flashed him a smile that looked pained. "It's stopped raining."

He looked around. "Indeed it has."

She pointed past him. "And there's even a rainbow." He turned and saw it, complete from end to end, arching ever the skyline in the distance. "Which means it's still raining somewhere." He looked back at the girl scout who was staring in the direction of the rainbow. She saw him looking at her and smiled at him again. This time the smile was fresh and spontaneous.

"So..." he began.

"Livvy." She held out her hand, which he shook gingerly.

"Raymond. So Livvy. You skipped

school because you needed to sell cookies?"

"Yep. And today's the last day. This afternoon I either turn in a whole wad of cash. Or I hand back this bag of cookies they gave me two weeks ago. Two weeks. Not one single box. Do you know how embarrassing that is? To not sell a single box? So I figured..." She looked around as if someone was eavesdropping. "I figured why not knock on some doors now. Catch some housewives – or househusbands – who are home alone and could use a good sugary snack right about now."

Raymond laughed. "You know, if you were one of my kids I'd say shame on you for skipping school."

Her laughter joined his. "Good thing I'm not then, huh?" So. Mr. Raymond..." Livvy stepped forward and held out her hand. "You wanna help me earn my 'help old folks across the street' badge?" Raymond slipped his hand into hers. "Sure. You can never have too many badges, right?"

"Right. Or, I guess, too many boxes of cookies." She gripped his hand firmly as he lowered first his cane and then his bum leg off the curb and into the crosswalk. With a person holding onto him, even a person as little as Livvy, Raymond was even more aware of how his body jerked to one side when he took a step. Or his feet as they drug across the pavement. It was an odd rhythm and didn't go with his heart pounding with exertion against his chest.

Livvy broke the silence. "So you mentioned kids?"

"Yes." Raymond nodded. "Children. I have children. Actually..." He paused in the middle of the crosswalk. Livvy took a step ahead of him and almost let go of his hand before stopping also. "Actually...child. as in one. A single child is what I have now."

Livvy gazed at him like she could see his fillings. She did not blink for a long time. She glanced over her shoulder and he saw past her at a yellow car approaching. He could usually tell the make and model just by the grill and the headlights, but there were so many new models nowadays. They continued their slow stepping to the opposite curb. Once they were out of the crosswalk and the yellow car honked on its way past (it was a Ford), Raymond pointed at a bench a little ways up the sidewalk. "Get me to there and I'll be good," he said. "If you don't mind. I just could rest for a little bit before I keep going."

"Sure thing." Livvy squeezed his hand and heaved the grocery bag higher in her one arm before they continued their walk.

Raymond was taking short, shallow breaths by the time they got there. Livvy let him step past her and he sagged onto the bench, gripping his cane between his knees. He tilted his head back and closed his eyes, trying to draw out his breaths. He could feel Livvy standing there looking at him. Finally she spoke.

"So your kid. Is it a boy or a girl?"

He lifted his head and opened his eyes to catch her gaze. The girl could sure look right through a person. "A girl...uh, a girl..." He hesitated. Using the word "girl" to describe his fifty-one year old daughter. "A woman actually..." The word "woman" landed like lead on the inside of his mouth. "But yeah. A girl I guess." He paused. "You remind me a lot of her actually. Really pretty at your age. And smart. So smart."

"A girl. Cool." Livvy sat down on the bench next to Raymond and sat the grocery bag on the ground in front of her. "Smart huh. She probably would've sold all her cookies by now." "Oh I don't know." Raymond shook his head. "She was interested in other things."

Suddenly she was very interested in the cookies as she reached into the bag and began shifting the boxes. "She had brothers...or sisters?" she asked, talking down into the bag.

Raymond watched her sorting for a moment before looking across the street at a tall brick building with a white spire and a cross on the front. "There was an older sister," he replied. "Penelope. Penny. She was a baby." The words started coming harder. "There was a complication at birth. She died. Cassie never knew her."

Livvy looked up and then buried her face back in the boxes. "She died?" The moving of the boxes got more intense. "I'm so sorry." Raymond nodded and his eyes hurt.

"And a brother." His voice cracked as he spoke. "She had a brother too."

All noise and activity with the boxers stopped. He could feel Livvy looking at him. A breath with sharp edges filled up his lungs and made a noise as it came out of his mouth.

"She had a brother. I had a son. Joe."

"Aaahhh..." he heard Livvy say. He glanced down and over at the same time. Now she was looking across the street. He followed her gaze and stared at the church. He tried to count the rows of brick on the front of the building. Counting meant not thinking. The two of them sat in silence, looking straight ahead.

Finally she sighed. "Cookies." She

looked over at Raymond. "I've got cookies to sell. And if I'm gonna miss school and risk getting bad grades in all my classes – neither of which my parents will notice by the way – then the least I can do is go sell some cookies. So you good?"

"Better than I deserve." Raymond smiled as she rummaged through her bag. "Okay…" she said. "Not sure what that means. But you know what you do deserve." She paused for effect as her hand emerged from the bag gripping a green box. "Cookies! They make everything better!" She expertly slid one finger along one end to open the box. She pulled out a sleeve of dark chocolate wafers that looked like thin mints, which she proffered to Raymond. "One for you…" She looked down into the box, "and one for me." Raymond paused for a second before taking the present. "How are you doing this? Don't you need to sell these?" Livvy winked at him before once again embracing the bag to her chest. "The cookies are six dollars a box. Well now…" She winked at him again. "Now they're seven."

And with that she turned and walked away.

Raymond could see her bounce as she walked. And why not? There were people who needed sugar. And she had girl scout cookies.

CHAPTER 9

After looking at her phone, Cassie scanned the waiting room, a process that took about eight and a half seconds. She didn't see her father anywhere. She had been gone much longer than she'd expected to – but maybe he was still back with the doctor. She pointed over to a row of chairs and Joey obediently skulked over and dropped himself into one. She walked over to the front desk where Moustache was bent over her keyboard. When Cassie got closer, however, she saw that Moustache wasn't working. She had both of her hands on a burrito the size of a St. Bernard's turd and was in the process of deep-throating it like a python. Cassie slowed her stride as she approached the desk, hoping the receptionist would bite off a chunk and chew for a minute before she asked her a question.

"So..." Cassie started. Moustache's eyes shot up to make contact though the rest of her body stayed curved over the keyboard. Cassie continued, working on keeping the edges of her mouth from turning upward. "My father. Raymond Chandler..."

Moustache held up a finger. And bit. And chewed. And swallowed. With the finger upright. And finally she spoke.

"Raymond?" She put down the dog turd burrito and turned to her computer screen, her fingers poised over the keys. "Chandler? Why does that sound..."

"Familiar? Yeah I know. It has that effect on people."

Moustache whispered the name again under her breath and tapped on the keys, her eyes scanning the screen in front of her. "Okay so...Raymond Chandler. He had an 8:30 with the doctor. But I haven't gotten his file back yet. He – the doctor – wanted to speak with you when you got here. So..." Her eyes leapt up to Cassie's face. "Maybe he's still back there with the doctor?"

"May. Be." Cassie drew out her response very slowly as if the receptionist was hard of hearing. "Why don't. You just go. Back there. And see."

Moustache blinked at her two or three times as if mentally processing. Then she slowly, almost in slow motion slow, got to her feet. She wiped her lap, checked it, then wiped again. She smacked her lips once like she still had food in her mouth before she spoke, again in slow motion. "I'll be right back," she said as she turned to walk away.

"Thanks so much," Cassie called after her. "Thanks for doing your job." She watched Moustache's back as the receptionist hesitated for a second. She hadn't disappeared through the door when Cassie turned and walked back to where Joey was sitting. He didn't have his ear buds in like he usually did however – instead he was looking right at her, something he almost never did. She slid into the seat next to him and his head pivoted in her direction. She couldn't read the look on his face because she had never seen it before.

"What?" she asked finally.

And still he stared at her. It took a few seconds to reply. "Mom, you're just mean," he said.

"What?"

"You heard me." At that he turned away from her and shoved the buds deep into his ears. She reached up and yanked them out by the white cord that attached them to his phone. "Yes, I heard you. But I can't believe what I heard. So I want to hear it again." She paused to let her message sink in. "So what did you say to me?"

"You're mean! Mom, you're so...so goddamn mean!" He was facing her now and was shouting in her face. The use of "goddamn" from him startled her and she pulled back, but he persisted, leaning in as he shouted at her. "You're...so...mean! All the time! To everyone! You're mean to me! You're mean to Grandpa! You were mean to that lady just now! And you don't even know her! Why?? Why are you so mean all the time??"

His voice rang in her ears and yet it seemed to come from far away. In her peripheral vision she could see the faces of other patients in the waiting room as they turned to look at the two of them. She opened her mouth and loved her lips but no words came. She felt her jaws working – this time she was the one chewing, though there was nothing in her mouth.

"Yeah. That's what I thought." Jory snatched the buds from her hand and crammed them back into his ears. He turned his body away from his mother and closed his eyes as the music filled his brain. Cassie's brain, on the other hand, had nothing. She continued to work her jaw and move her lips. "Mean. I am mean," she said.

"Yes. I am mean. In fact, I am downright nasty." She repeated the same words over and over again. As far as words went, that's all she had. But in terms of pictures, there were more than she could handle. Images blossomed into full memories, blooming and growing and turning around her, dark and dangerous and yet somehow bleakly beautiful, and she knew that the monstrous that threatened to envelope her back in the principal's office didn't totally disappear. She had managed to mainly hold it at bay for a hot second, but now it was back and this time it would not be satisfied until it totally consumed her. The monster spread out its vines and blocked out all the light in the waiting room. She could see nothing and no one.

Except, at first, Lloyd. Ah yes, she thought as she struggled to squint through the darkness, why not start there. When she was fifteen years old and she said yes when she didn't really want to. Good old Lloyd, with the round face and the dumb smile. Lloyd, who wore cowboy boots to school every day and added an extra little kick to his stride, like his penis had brushed against the side of his leg as he walked and he needed to brush it off before he took the next step. He had invaded her personal space that day – she had closed her locker and there he was, with his round face and his goody grin, giving her no place to look. He'd asked her to go to the prom that day – he was a senior after all – and their mothers walked together every day. She was sure that was where the whole idea had started. So she told him she'd think about it, but the next day she said yes.

    She didn't remember much about the prom itself. She wore a pink miniskirt with white flowers, which was unheard of for a prom. But she had great legs, even as a teenager, so why not? At one point she had had enough of Lloyd and snuck outside for a cigarette. This was when Dwight's face replaced Lloyd's in the fog and darkness that surrounded her. Dwight, who looked like Robert Redford – tall and lean and blonde with blue eyes that could memorize the details of her face before she even knew it was being studied. He walked up to her outside and asked her out because "if you said yes to Lloyd then I figured I had a chance." She said yes, this time without thinking. She was so ready to be loved by someone besides her brother, or her parents (who could be so maddeningly inconsistent with displays of affection). And he was good to her, and kind. And she was happy. She was open to all possibilities. Perhaps too open, since there was a pregnancy. And an abortion. And a screaming match with her mother once she found out. That was when she first noticed her upper register, utilized most often in times of stress.

But then her brother Joe, just two years younger and brimming with adoration for her, was gone. And then dead. And suddenly it was as if she never knew what happiness felt like. She dropped out of nursing school after her freshman year "because it was too hard." But not before the very notion of love began to taste bad on the inside of her mouth. And certainly not before a smile from a boy in the hallway of her dorm was all the charm she needed to not think straight. He had the same youthful waste about him as the young Keith Richards, and two months later they were sitting on the couch at her parent's house announcing that they'd eloped earlier that day. It seemed like a good idea at the time, especially in those moments when he was inside her and she was pulling his hair and her breath hitched in her throat. Raymond and Joanne were considerably less enthused, especially since they were still getting used to Dwight, the grand defiler of their only daughter, as a potential son-in-law. A few too many verbal arguments turning into slaps across the face from her chronically under-employed husband and she came to see their point of view. There was not another baby, so after four years it was easiest to walk away.

By that time she was working as a receptionist at a medical center (I'm mean to Moustache because she is me, Cassie thought briefly), the only job she could get in the medical profession without a degree. Weekly trips to church with her parents had, over time, been replaced with weekly trips to her favorite neighborhood watering hole. Communion wine had been switched out for whatever was on tap and two for one at happy hour. The one thing she missed about church, however, was looking at the stained glass window of Jesus above the alter. When the sun shone through the colored panes the whole thing glowed. And that was something she could really get behind. He cradled a lamb in his arms like it was a baby and he looked like he would be kind to everyone. Plus, he had a great beard.

So when the new bartender at her favorite bar passed her a Bud Light and the foam spilled over onto his hand, she took note. Now there was Aaron lighting up the darkness of her memories, bearded and with a kind face like stained-glass Jesus. He looked like the last person to slap you across the face. And he was ambitious. He worked construction during the week and bartended on the weekends because he wanted stuff – a car, a house, a wife – and the middle-class lifestyle that came with it. She promised herself that this time she would take her time. But there was something inside her, hard to describe, that was struggling to get out, and before she knew it she had a ring on her finger again.

What started off very healthy died a very slow painful death. Like cancer, something invisible ate away at the marriage. By the time she discovered MySpace, and discovered you could talk to people online when there was no talking going on at home, it was essentially dead. There was a lot of stuff, including a house with a pool, which her father helped finance. Meanwhile, Aaron worked less and less construction. His back hurt him, he said, though he never went to the doctor. Not so suddenly, he was just a bartender. Gray appeared in his beard so he shaved it. He no longer looked like Jesus. He worked when she was home, and was home and asleep when she was working. And there was still no baby. Perhaps her womb had been angry and clenched for so long that she was sterile. Or too stubborn to conceive.

People at work told her about a new web-site where you could connect with people. Find old friends. And even though she didn't feel like she had any friends, they had a computer in the house (Aaron had insisted on that as well). So there it sat, in the corner of the living room. As soon as she sat down in front of it, however, she suspected her husband used it quite a bit since some of the keys were shinier than others. She found the site easily enough. But then she paused. She couldn't think of anyone to look up. She typed in her father's name. Not surprisingly, nothing came up. Her husband – also not surprisingly, his profile did come up. Lots of pictures of himself. None of her. A couple people from work. Of course, since they suggested it.

And then she thought of Dwight. Her hands shook as she typed in his name.

And there he was. He still had all of his blonde hair. He had wrinkles around his eyes and those lines from his nose to his mouth. But his blue eyes were looking at the camera, and the observer, like he totally understood what he was seeing. Her fingers still shaking, she thought for a second and then typed. "Hi Dwight. This is Cassie from high school. We almost had a baby."

His answer came minutes later. "We did. I remember."

That was September. In November Aaron moved out, taking his computer with him, and Dwight moved in. And in January, two months shy of her 43rd birthday, Cassie's period was late for the first time since she was nineteen. Maybe her womb wasn't so clenched and angry after all.

"Mom." Joey's voiced sliced through the vines and branches and blossoms. The monstrous dark thing spread out and away from Cassie's body, flying into the corners of the room where it hovered and watched and waited. There was suddenly so much light that Cassie blinked and blinked again, but still could see nothing.

"Mom?"

She turned in the direction of the voice. Joey was staring at her, and not for the first time she saw Dwight in him. She blinked again. He pointed and she looked up at Moustache and the doctor, who were standing over her. They both looked like they were about to throw up.

"May we speak to you?" The doctor asked. She kept blinking. "Back in my office please?" He continued.

"What?" She looked back and forth

between the two of them and her son. Joey leaned in. "Mom," he whispered. "I think they lost Grandpa."

"Wh-what?" Her head kept up the pivot. "What about Grandpa?"

The doctor put his hand on her shoulder. "Is she okay?" Moustache asked.

"Yes, she's fine," Joey countered, standing up to face her. He reached out and took both hands in his, bending down to look her directly in the face. "The doctor wants to talk to you back in his office. Come on Mom," he said, so gently that she flinched. She stood and allowed herself to be led from the waiting room. The receptionist returned to her desk, and the doctor went ahead and held the door for Cassie. Joey put his arm around her and leaned his body into hers. She looked around as she walked. Everyone was in some kind of great hurry to return to whatever they were doing. And over in the corner, the dark monstrous thing hovered, waiting to pounce again.

CHAPTER 10

The bench where Raymond sat was like his bed – he had to gather his considerable reserves of energy to push off and stand. He scooted to the edge of the bench and put out his cane squarely in front of him. He gripped the top of the cane with both hands and began to push down, while at the same time willing the rest of his body upward.

Just then the front doors to the church across the street slammed open. Three couples hurried through, arms locked. They separated as soon as they cleared the doorway. The three women were all dressed alike in pale shimmery blue gowns and flowers in their hair. The men were also similarly dressed in grey suits and bowties. Their shirts were obviously meant to match the dresses. They were all young and flushed and glowing and happy. The group turned to look back into the dark gaping mouth of the church which, in order to please them, spit out another couple. These two were different. The woman was all in white, with a veil folded away from her face. The man had a black tuxedo and a white shirt. The woman carried a small bouquet of flowers. Behind them the church continued to vomit out people, way too many to count. They were all dressed, as Joanne would have said, in their Sunday-go-to-meeting clothes.

Joanne. He would like to have said she looked beautiful in her wedding dress as she walked down the aisle of their church on their wedding day – what was it, almost fifty years ago now? – but really, she just looked like Joanne all dressed up. She had dieted for months before she could fit into a size six, even though he preferred her with more curves. He had only had one other serious girlfriend, the girl next door who rode to school every day with Raymond and his brothers in the family Ford and sat in the back seat with Raymond. When he graduated from high school and that ended and he seemed in no hurry to replace her, there was some concern in the church community that it would never happen. And then he was drafted and away for two years and when he came back, and still there was no beau. And he was almost twenty-two. It wasn't his grouchy mother, who would instantly dislike anyone anyway, who picked out Joanne for him. Rather it was his aunt, a loud vulgar woman, who pointed her out, the only daughter of neighbors two miles down the road, as Joanne was getting out of the car with her parents one day. Almost twenty-one and not married. Graduated from high school and working for a local doctor – like mother like daughter as it turned out. And so he studied her as she sat in a pew across the aisle from him. So intent on what was going on during the service. And not smiling. And following along as the pastor read from the Bible, her finger travelling along the passages. He saw her lips moving as she read to herself. The truth was that everything that happened to him in his life so far – the first girlfriend, the military service, the farming – happened because it came to him. Clearly he was going to have to travel in this direction in order for anything to happen. She acted like she wasn't even aware of him, even though they had gone to the same church since birth.

 So after the service he went up and spoke to her. Her eyes behind her dark-rimmed glasses searched his face as he spoke, as if looking for another meaning behind his words. But a week later she went with him to a chili supper at another church. A weekly thing became two or three times a week. Sometimes they went out – but the tiny little town they lived in only had two or three restaurants, depending on the month, and one theater that played movies that had already been out for a year. Joanne's family was one of the first in town to own a color television, so more and more Raymond would come over to Joanne's house and watch "Gunsmoke" and other shows they liked. Raymond loved TV and before he knew it he loved Joanne. The couch in the living room was long for a tall adult man to sleep on, and at first Raymond and Joanne sat at opposite ends with their elbows on the arm rests. But gradually, as the Sheriff and Miss Kitty flirted on TV, the space on the couch between them got smaller and smaller until their fingers were touching between them. One night her parents went to bed early and he turned to her. He could feel her breath on her cheek. And that, as they say, was that.

Across the street in front of him a spectacle was unfolding. The crowd of Sunday-go-to-meeting folk had clustered in groups on the grass, leaving the sidewalk for the wedding party. The bride had hitched up her dress. The groom was kneeling in front of her and she put her leg on his knee. He reached for a garter on her thigh and slowly inched it off her leg, winking and smiling the whole time. Without looking behind him, he tossed it over his shoulder to the three groomsmen huddled a short distance behind him. An impossibly long arm from the tallest one, perhaps someone who played basketball in high school, reached up and snatched it out of the air. There followed a litany of laughter between the three men and the groom, who had turned around to look.

Next it was the bride's turn. She turned her back to the bridesmaids who giggled as they switched places with the groomsmen. She swung the bouquet one, two, three times before throwing her arms over her head and tossed the flowers behind her to the women in pink. Shrieks were followed by arms flailing in the air, but the bouquet bounced off the fingers of the women in front and landed in the arms of the one who lingered behind the other two. She was short and petite and blonde and she looked startled by the unexpected gift she was holding. The other two screamed and hugged her, but her expression remained confused and unsure.

After that the crowd dispersed quickly. A limo pulled up and away with the bride and groom. People walked down the sidewalk. The groomsmen and bridesmaids paired off and headed away. Only the one with the bouquet stayed standing on the sidewalk, looking down at the flowers like she'd just been handed a strange baby. The basketball player with the garter hesitated by her side and whispered something in her ear. She shook her head without looking up and he sauntered off down the sidewalk twirling the garter on his finger. The bridesmaid stood where he left her, looking down at the flowers until everyone else had left. She shook her head again and her arms dropped to her sides. The bouquet slipped from her fingers to the ground. She stood for a minute looking out in front of her. She dabbed at her eyes and hurried after her groomsmen. The flowers stayed behind, a splash of color on the sidewalk.

    Raymond was so involved in what was going on across the street that he forgot he was perched on the edge of the bench. His hands remained perched on the top of his cane. He watched the pink dress as it scurried away out of view before he returned to the task at hand. Pushing down with his hands, he propelled the rest of his body upward with more force than he was used to. He staggered forward and only at the last moment caught himself from toppling over. He stood and breathed deeply, trying to imagine what the disease inside him looked like. He imagined it had fingers that it wrapped around the air as it came out of his lungs and squeezed it away.

    He put his cane into the street and followed after it, hobbling across the street and looking both ways. He glanced down at the flowers on his way past but didn't want to stop, not yet. The very sight of the flowers on the sidewalk were almost more than he could handle. The heavy wooden doors were also almost more than he could handle, but once he pried them open, he was hit with cold air conditioning that made him sigh.

    He was standing in the sanctuary where just a little while ago a woman in white wedding dress marched her way down the aisle towards what she almost definitely thought was a certain future. The church looked like every other – red carpet, rows of smooth wooden pews, stained glass windows along the walls, alter in the front, Jesus on the cross above it. Women in patterned dresses walked briskly among the rows of pews, plucking up wads of flowers off the ends facing the aisle and picking programs off the seats. Joanne would have called them church ladies. Like his mother. And his loud aunt. He surveyed his surroundings. It was always so quiet inside churches. Voices echoed and then died, covered over by silence. Thoughts formed inside your head and then disappeared, pushed out by silence. As a kid he often told his parents he liked going to church because he loved Jesus. But the truth of the matter was that he enjoyed the silence, thick as smoke in the air. He closed his eyes and listened to nothing.

"Sir? Can I help you?"

The voice cut through the quiet. He turned slowly towards the sound, thinking to himself that most people should really know better than to sneak up on old men who might have bad hearts. The man smiling back at him looked friendly and kind. Lots of beard and a shaved head gave his face a bottom-heavy appearance. Cassie would have liked that. His arm rested on a vacuum. Raymond couldn't imagine how he didn't hear all of that sneaking up on him.

"Excuse me. I didn't mean to startle you." The bearded man continued.

"You didn't..."

His hand shot out to Raymond. "Mike. Mike Sweeney. I'm the janitor here." He gestured at the vacuum. "Are you here for the wedding? If so, you just missed it." He gestured around him to the sanctuary.

Raymond shook his head. "I'm not here for the wedding." Mike immediately looked sheepish. He had a great bottom-heavy face. His feelings were always just right there. "Okay...Well did you need to see the pastor? The regular one is sick I'm afraid. A guest pastor performed the ceremony, but he's gone already."

The old man reached up and rubbed his nose. "Nah. I'm not here to see the reverend either." Mike cocked his head to one side like he was waiting for something. "Is there something I can..."

"I'm not sure why I'm here, to be perfectly honest with you." Raymond interrupted him. His voice quavered as he spoke. "I guess it just felt like this was where I was supposed to be. At this moment in time."

Mike's head snapped back upright. "Water." He said. "I'll bet you could use some water." Raymond licked his lips and nodded. "Yeah. Water would be good right about now." Mike looked around and pointed to a pew behind them. "Here. Why don't you sit right here. I'll be right back." But he hesitated, watching, as Raymond went through the elaborate dance of getting his body to sit. Once Mike was gone Raymond looked around. The church ladies had finished their duties and left. He was alone in the sanctuary. He looked up over the alter at Christ on the cross. There was so much detail to the figure – you could see the ribs and the muscles beneath the skin. Jesus' face was twisted in an agony – the mouth was open and the eyes were rolled upwards. Perhaps he was calling out to God. Father figure me perhaps?

Mike was back by his side, twisting the cap off a bottle of water and handing it to him. Raymond tipped the bottle farther than he should have and water ran down his cheeks as he gulped deeply several times. He gasped as he finished and his hand shook as he handed the bottle back to Mike. He wiped his mouth and looked back over the alter.

"It's a shrine to suffering isn't it?" He said.

"What? It's what?" Mike flinched.

"I just figured it out. Just now. It's all about the suffering. They put an image of pain right up front. And then they put the chairs, the pews, whatever..." Raymond waved his arm all around them. "They put the seats all facing in that direction so that we all have to look at it."

Mike looked up above the alter and then back at the old man. "So I'm guessing you're familiar with the phrase 'Christ suffered for your sins'?"

Raymond nodded. "Oh yeah. I've heard that phrase many a time. Many a time."

He nodded his head. "If you hear it enough times, it almost doesn't sound like words anymore."

Mike held up his finger. "Hold on. I'll be right back. I have something I want to give you."

And he was gone. He was a fast one, that Mike. And he was back before Raymond knew it, clutching pamphlets in his hands. He slid into the pew next to the old man and held out his hand with the brochures in them. The words DO YOU BELIEVE? Were spelled out in white letters above a photo of a sun either going down or coming up over the horizon. Probably coming up, if Raymond had to guess.

"I want to give you one of these to take with you. Wait. Hold on. This one is ripped…" Mike held up a pamphlet. The cover had a tear through BELIEVE. He began to rifle through the stack for an un-mangled one. "No wait. That's good. I'll take that one." Raymond reached out and took the torn brochure from between Mike's fingers. He folded it along the tear and tucked it in his pocket. "And now…" He said as he began to elaborate process which, for him, was standing. "It's time for me to get going. I need to get home."

"Miles to go before you sleep, right?" Mike said with a smile. Then he added, when Raymond looked at him, "No. Nothing. Never mind. Here, let me help you." And he slipped his arm expertly under the old man's elbow. Once they had cleared the pew he jogged ahead to open the door. "Very nice to meet you...uh..."

"Raymond."

"Raymond. Very nice to see you. Hope we get to see you here on Sunday. Services start at ten. You're welcome anytime."

He stood with one hand holding the door open and the other hand out to shake with Raymond. Things had become oddly, and suddenly, formal. Mike kept looking down at the ground as if now not knowing what else to say besides responses he knew by heart. He hesitated, looked up and smiled at Raymond. Then he was gone and the heavy door sighed closed behind him.

Raymond turned and blinked in the sun. After being in the air conditioning, it felt really warm outside. He hobbled toward the bouquet, which still lay discarded and lonely in the middle of the sidewalk. As he got closer, he could see a bee fly from blossom to blossom. He bent over to shoo it away before picking it up. His bones made popping sounds as he straightened up. Some of the flowers, already wilted in the heat, drifted through his fingers to the ground, but most of the bunch held together. Joanne would have known the names of each and every one, though for a farmer he was surprisingly ignorant of flowers. He could pick out tulips and daisies and roses, but that was about it. He usually called them by their colors – the purple ones, the red ones, the pink ones. He put them to his face and inhaled deeply. The smell was so sweet he could almost taste it. He shifted the bouquet to the hand without the cane and colors continued to drop through his fingers. He thought briefly about picking them up – but the very thought of bending over again wore him out. And right now he needed all the strength he could muster. What was it that Mike said? Miles to go before you sleep?

Indeed.

CHAPTER 11

Once again the inside of the car was quiet as a church – or at least churches before they added guitars and rock music and amplification and video. Cassie was so lost in thought that she barely noticed. She was making a mental list of everything she did once she was told her father was missing:

Immediately calling him on his cell phone. But he never turned it on, and even if he did he never carried it with him. She had a feeling that when they got home and went into his room it would be sitting right there on his bedside table. What a waste of money that was;

She then called the police. A missing old man didn't have the same sense of urgency that a school shooting did, so it seemed to take forever for them to get to the hospital. Though they probably arrived in fifteen minutes;

They asked questions. Lots of questions. Did he drive? Were there other relatives living locally who would have come to pick him up? Would he have taken an Uber or taxi to another location for any reason? Considering his recent diagnosis – Cassie heard about it mere minutes before the police did - was he the kind of person who would consider harming himself? Did she know of anyone who might want to hurt her father? Had he spoken earlier in the day about wanting or needing to go someplace else besides the doctor? Would he have accepted a ride from someone he didn't know? There were so many;

They asked what he looked like. No one carried pictures in their wallet anymore, so she sent one to them electronically;

They studied security footage from the hospital. They saw him walking through the hall with the doctor and sitting in the waiting room. Suddenly, for him, he was standing and out the door. So at least he left the facility of his own accord;

They asked them to go home (they started with "the best way you can help right now is…," which made her want to slap them) and they would be in touch as soon as they knew something. Which was what they were doing now.

"Do you think Grandpa's okay?" The silence cracked around her. She glanced over at her son, who didn't have the buds in his ears. That was not a good sign. It meant he actually wanted to talk for a change.

"Huh?" She asked, gripping the wheel tighter. She had heard perfectly what he said.

"Grandpa," Joey repeated. "Do you think he's okay."

"You mean beside the whole dying thing?"

"Mom..."

"Sorry. I...sorry..." She concentrated on the road because she really didn't have an answer. But she tried. "He's old. And he's tired. And sick. And lonely as hell. His world is getting smaller and smaller. And the world he is in is totally strange to him. Nothing here is familiar to him in any way. Not even me. Or you." She paused to let all that sink in. "So no. I'd say he's not okay. Probably not. Not anywhere close to okay."

Huge silence answered her from over on Joey's side of the car. She darted her eyes in his direction. He was chewing his lips so there was more.

"How about you?" He asked after a

minute. "Are you okay?"

She snorted, trying to sound devil-may-care, but the end of the sound had a choked quality to it, like it was drowning in water. "Define okay."

"You know what okay means. Okay. All right. Fine..." He struggled for adjectives. "You know...happy."

That time she laughed out loud. "That, my friend, is two entirely different things. Okay is a long, long way off from happy." She contemplated for a minute. "Am I okay?" Sure. I guess I am. I mean, I'm not dead. Or dying. Or starving. Or living on the street. So yeah, I guess I'm okay. But am I happy? Now that is the million dollar question. Am I happy?" She paused and sighed, even though she already knew the answer. "Well let's see. Alright...I don't have much of a career to speak of. I mean, I answer phones for a living. I have two ex-husbands, and the third one, well..." She paused for a second as something dark passed across her field of vision. "I have a teenager who got in trouble for fighting at school. Which..." She was quick to add, since she could hear him start to speak, "is the least of my worries right now. And to top it all off, I have a father with cancer who has somehow managed to disappear off the face of the earth." She glanced over in his direction again before returning her eyes to the road. "So does that sound to you like the kind of rosy little picture I would draw for myself with my Crayola crayons when I was a little girl?" Out of the corner of her eye she saw him shake his head. She nodded. "You're right. It doesn't. Not one little bit. I can't even draw the H on that picture with the kind of life I've been having."

    She paused. She was about to drown swimming towards this thing that she had never said before. The dark monstrous thing couldn't be far behind. Her voice sounded odd as she spoke. "So no. I guess I'm not happy. Not at all. Not one little bit." She felt deflated. Exhausted. It was all she could do to focus on driving, though it felt like she was physically pushing the car up the street. "Bitter. Party of one. That's what they say when I walk into a restaurant. If I could ever afford to go to a restaurant."

    The joke landed with a thud on the seat between them. He obviously didn't get it. His mouth was open, so maybe he didn't even hear it and was instead working through something else in his head.

    "Oh honey." She reached over and put her hand on his head. Like when she held him as a baby, she hoped he could feel her pulse and her heat and it would calm him. Earlier the intimacy had surprised her. This time she reached for the action like she was thirsty and needed to drink deep. He didn't flinch like he usually did – rather he tilted his head into her hand and stayed. This was easier than words, she thought, her fingers laced through his curls and resting lightly on his skull.

"The first time ever I saw your face..."

Roberta Flack was suddenly everywhere around her in the car. For a hot second it felt like she was in a movie and she had a soundtrack. Which prompted a "What the fu..." Until she realized that Roberta was in her purse.

"I thought the sun rose in your eyes..."

She kept one hand on the wheel and took the other off Joey's head to plunge into the chaos that was her hand bag. By the time she'd fished her cell out it had gone to voice mail so she held it in front of her. She was expecting a call. Or maybe it was the police. But she didn't recognize the number. When she called back, the voice on the other end was deep and booming. Be the police she on the screen to call them back. The voice on the other end was deep and booming.

"This is Bennie."

Her mind drew a blank. "Bennie? Bennie, who?"

"The orderly at the hospital. You know, the one who carried your father."

And suddenly her mind was no longer blank. Bennie. Big guy. Big muscles. Great smile. Nice guy. "I got your number from the hospital records. I hope you don't mind." He hardly waited for a response. "I heard about your dad. I just wanted to see if you'd heard anything yet." Her urge was to snap back I just left the hospital of course I haven't heard anything yet. But her son's voice, a memory from earlier, laid in her ear and stopped her. You're mean Mom. And behind that, underneath and still but still present was his voice again. Flirt much? She breathed deep.

"No. I don't mind at all. And nothing yet."

"Listen. I'm at my other job. You have my number now. If there is anything I can do for you, please, please let me know."

It was when she hung up and was shoving the cell back into her bag that she saw the flash of black and white to the left outside on the road. Something passed under the front wheel on her side and she looked in the rear view mirror just in time to see the body of the cat fly into the air behind the car. She screamed and hit the brakes so hard that Joey's face flew towards the dash. The brakes screeched and the vehicle was still lurching forward when she flew open the door and ran back to where the cat was flipping its body up into the air and back down onto the road. She sunk to her knees and watched the animal, desperate in its death throes. She could only imagine the cat wasn't expecting to go so soon or so suddenly and was no doubt trying to hold onto something that was slipping away despite its best efforts. The flopping grew less and less and by the time Joey walked up behind his mother the cat had heaved itself half off the pavement and was still. Her shoulders were jerking as she sobbed.

"Motherfucker," she said over and over again.

"Mom..." There was a gentleness to his voice she had never heard before. He put his hand on her shoulder. "Mom. It's a dead cat. You didn't mean to kill it."

She put her head in her hands. She too felt like she was trying to hold onto something that was slipping away. "It's always a dead cat. Or two. Or twelve." She said from behind her hands. "And you never mean to kill it." She almost howled the last words.

She stood. "My phone," she gasped.

"I've got to get my phone." She staggered in the direction of the car. And suddenly Joey was in front of her. He reached out and took hold of her arms.

"Mom. Please no. Mom…" She looked past him to the car. "He's going to call. He said…"

"Mom!" Joey's hands let go of her arms and cupped her face, making her look at him. "Look at me. Dad's dead. He drove off and he died. I know he said he'd call but he won't. He's dead. It's been a year. He won't call. And you've got to stop waiting."

"What?" She stared at her son and wiped her eyes – and for a second, the father not the son stood in front of her. And she heard the last words he said to her, "I'll call you when I get there," before he drove away and had a heart attack from too much drinking and smoking and ran into a pole and died. And even though she saw the body and attended the service, the grief was cutting huge jagged chunks out of her heart. The only thing that filled the holes was hitting rewind and replay and hearing his voice making a promise.

    I'll call you when I get there
    I'll call you when I
    I'll call you
    And she waited.

And waited.

She wiped her eyes again. Her husband's face faded into Joey's.

"He's gone Mom. He's not going to call." And then he did something he hadn't done since he was nine years old. He put his arm around her. Then he was so little that his tiny fingers gripped her waist. Now, on his knees next to his mother, he was almost the same size so that his arm rested lightly across her shoulders. This time it was she who was feeling the heat of his body through his skin. It was immensely calming. She sniffled and wiped her nose.

"Mom," he whispered into her ear. "I love you, you know that right? But..." and he leaned in closer. "Your metaphors really need some work. That analogy really sucks. You know that right?"

She laughed despite herself. He joined her, a sound so golden and beautiful and unusual that she folded herself into him and put her head against his chest. Let someone else's beating heart feel things for a change.

"We must look a sight," she said. "Two people kneeling in the middle of the street praying to a dead cat."

They came apart. The moment was done but lingered in the air. Joey looked down at the cat corpse. "You know we can't leave it here," he said. "True," she agreed. "Well, you help your old mother up off her knees. I think I have a garbage bag in the trunk."

He stood before her, holding his hand out to her. He pulled her to her feet and they walked back to the car. She limped at first because her knees ached. He held her hand the whole time.

CHAPTER 12

Raymond counted his progress in city blocks. If he made it to the end of the block he could rest for a minute. But blocks became half blocks and half blocks became squares of sidewalk. Eventually he couldn't go a few feet without losing his breath. It felt like someone was sitting on his chest.

Up ahead, halfway down the block, was a bus stop. If he could get that far he would rest for a minute. Maybe he would get on the next bus so he could ride for a while, though he wouldn't necessarily know where it was going. He could ask. He just really needed to sit. He would figure the rest later. He began counting steps. Or rather, every time he slid his foot forward – which for him counted as a step. It became like a sort of rhythm, putting his cane forward, it tapping the ground, and his feet dragging behind it one at a time. Between that and the frequent pauses to catch his breath, he found that he was making a weird kind of music.

Finally, he made it to the bench. The newer bus stops had plexi-glass and metal seats and maps on the side of the various bus routes drawn out in colored arrows. This was not one of them. Wooden slats long overdue for painting were balanced between concrete slabs that served for legs. The back of the bench advertised the number of a personal injury attorney with an unpronounceable last name. Raymond sat hard with his back to the attorney's face. All the air left his body. He felt as he was deflating.

The sun felt so good on his face. He tilted his head up and closed his eyes. If only he could stay here for a while and soak up the heat. Let things drift away, or come to him, for a change. Just sit still and see what happens. But the instant he had the thought he felt an unease with it. Ever since Joanne he had intentionally or not headed towards things. For better or for worse, which didn't just apply to marriage. As a matter of fact, applied to a whole lot more than just marriage. At this point he wouldn't know how to do it otherwise. Though maybe that was the problem. Maybe he should have done otherwise. Who knew. This dueling inside his brain was exhausting him and all he wanted to do was rest his body and feel the sun on his face.

He opened his eyes and looked to his left to see if a bus was coming. There was no big vehicle heading in his direction but there was a single person walking down the sidewalk that caught Raymond's attention. The rain had left the air very humid and the heat rose off the sidewalk. The person seemed to have a hitch to his step as he walked towards Raymond, almost as if he favored one side of his body. The old man tried not to stare, though it felt like he was seeing some other version of himself walking. Finally, he looked down and studied his hands, rubbing the fingers of one hand along the veins standing out on the other, waiting for the man to pass.

He felt the thud as the man collapsed onto the bench next to Raymond. There settled around the two of them, besides the thick oppressive heat, a silence equally thick. Raymond always felt that if two people were so close to each other physically that the least they should do is talk to each other. Otherwise it was just ignoring each other, which was rude. But Raymond had never been very comfortable in anything even vaguely resembling social situations, and people's recent obsession with their own cell phones had, thankfully, relieved him of the obligation to engage. Besides, there was pressure in his chest – had been for a while now. And now that it had a name it filled more and more of his thoughts. Everything about his ailing body did actually, but this one took the most space in his brain. Since this morning anyway. He felt like he had started a race with it to somewhere. So he inhaled and exhaled deeply, trying to breathe through it. The other man on the bench finally broke the silence.

"Has the number 8 been by yet?"

Raymond turned and looked at him for the first time. He looked physically young but mentally rough around the edges. He wore his sandy hair shaved close to his skull though his stubble was beginning to grow out on his face. His head was tucked down into the collar of his over-sized green jacket. He had dog-tags around his neck. His stained hands rubbed up and down the denim on his legs. He spoke again without looking up.

"Number 8 is the one I need. The one I ride. Do you know if the number 8 has come by yet?"

Raymond sighed. Breathe through the tumor. Breathe past the cancer. Breathe.

"Actually, I just got here myself. So no bus so far. Is the number 8 the bus that stops here?" The hands rubbing across denim sped up. "Yeah. The number 8 is the one I catch here every day."

Okay. This was good. This was the start of a conversation. "I don't know the buses here very well. Not yet. Sometimes I just get on one and ride." Which technically wasn't a lie since he randomly got onto a bus just this morning. Even though he had someplace he wanted to be. "Where does the 8 go to?"

"The VA. I go to the VA every day."

Breathe through. Breathe through. Breathe.

"Oh. You're a vet?"

"Yep. Two tours in Iraq." He held up three fingers. "Injured with a month to go in the second tour." He made the sound of a gigantic explosion, lifting his arms off his legs to make a large circular movement in the air. "Piece of metal the size of…" He looked around to find something the right size but settled on holding his thumb and finger about an inch apart and out to Raymond. "About the size of this buried in my skull. Shrapnel in my back. So close to my spine I could've been paralyzed. Shattered my pelvis. I'm a mess."

Raymond watched the young man intently. He seemed to relax into the conversation. Once he got going the hitch and jerkiness was gone. There was something delicate about the way his arms moved. But as Raymond watched, he began to slow down. "Yeah. A real mess is what I am." And with that his whole body ground to a halt. His hands dropped to his lap, his head bent down and he began to cry.

If Raymond felt uncomfortable before in the presence of silence, he felt downright embarrassed around crying. He reached out to touch the young man's arm but then stopped, reining in the instinct before it took him where he didn't want to go. He let his hand drop to the bench and looked at it as he listened to gasps and sniffles coming from the other end of the bench. Once it sounded like it was dying down, he reached over and extended his hand. Some physical contact would be better than nothing.

"Raymond Chandler by the way. I know. The name of a famous writer." The young man wiped his hand across his nose and grabbed Raymond's hand and shook it, his hand shaking as he shook. Raymond noticed the hand was wet. Breathe through. Breathe through. Breathe.

"I wouldn't know." Besides the shaking, his grip was strong. He continued to sniffle. "I don't read." He started the handshake up again so vigorously that Raymond thought his arm would vibrate out of its socket. "Bill here. Bill Williams. Yep you got that right. The first and last name's the same. Except for that one little S at the end. William Williams actually. But you can call me Bill. Or Billy. Or what-the-fuck-ever you want." And then he dropped Raymond's hand as if it had burned him and returned his own hands to his lap, palms down, and began to rub his jeans again. One leg started to bounce. It looked to Raymond as if Bill had multiple rhythms going on at the same time.

"So Raymond Chandler named after a famous writer I never heard of," Bill continued, looking to the left and the right but never directly at Raymond, "You ever been in the army?"

Raymond looked out and away from Bill. It was obvious it was going to be a no-eye-contact kind of conversation. And he was fine with that. Except for Joanne, he was always better not looking people directly in the eyes. "Yes. Yes I was." He nodded his head more than was absolutely necessary. "But it was between the wars so I didn't see combat."

"Didn't see combat eh?" That caught Bill's attention and for a brief second he looked right at Raymond. "Lucky you. Which wars you talking about?" He looked over at Raymond and squinted as he studied him. "I'm guessing Korea and Nam." He said "Nam" like "nod" which made Raymond happy and he smiled. "Yes, you're right. Between Korea and Vietnam. Very good."

"No combat though, huh? Then where'd they put you?"

"I was stationed in Germany. Behind a desk. In an office."

"In an office. Huh." Bill shook his head. The rubbing and bouncing sped up again. "I can't even imagine what that must've been like. I knew some guys who tested out and did that. Not me. Not smart enough. So I was in the field. And I don't think I need to tell you, it sucked to high heaven." He paused for a moment and his hands went up to his head. "When I was a kid we had this minister from Korea come and talk to our class at school. Never forget it. He survived the war. And he kept saying, over and over again, 'War is hair. War is hair.' Or at least that's what I thought I heard because he had an accent. Dumb stupid kid. I don't know what I was thinking. But I figured out much later that what he was saying was 'War is hell. War is hell.' But by then it was too late. I was already over there. But he was sure enough right. It was hell. A hell like you couldn't imagine."

Bill bent his head into his chest and wiped his face with his hands. Raymond watched him closely. Breathe through it. Breathe through it. Breathe. He listened to himself, but he didn't hear it. Something was rising in him, something he was unable to contain. He was going to drown.

Breathe through it.
Breathe through it.
Breathe...

"My son was in the army." He gasped as he spoke and he choked off the end of the sentence. "For a little while." All movement on the bench stopped and Bill turned to look at him. Raymond couldn't get enough air into his lungs. "For a little while I had a son. And for a little while he was in the army."

"You had a son." From Bill it was more of a statement.

"Yes." Raymond could feel the wet on his cheeks. It was already down to the edge of his mouth and he could taste it but he didn't care. "Joseph. Joe. He was such a good buy. I know everyone says that about their children, but in this case it was true. So kind to everyone. Smiled at...oh his smile...it was something else. And if he ever found an injured animal he would pick it up and hold it. And cry. Oh he could cry. Until long after it had died and we had to take it away from him. Even worms. Because he knew...he knew that that little piece of life was valuable." Raymond swallowed hard. His mouth, indeed his whole face, felt too wet. "Didn't like farming at all. Trudged behind me like I was asking him to march to his death. Couldn't drive a tractor to save his life. Lifting or carrying or digging...not his thing at all. But get a book from his mother and he would disappear for hours. And you'd find him under a tree or in his room. And the book was almost finished."

"He didn't have many friends, even at church. We asked him to bring people over. Maybe he was ashamed us. I don't know. But he did. Such a good boy, doing what he's told. Doing what he's told. Went on a few dates. People came over to study. Eventually there was a best friend." Raymond gulped. He wasn't sure Bill was even sitting next to him, but this was rising up out of him so fast that it didn't matter. "What good words those are. Best. Friend. Larry was his name. I think. Or Gary. I don't remember exactly. And eventually they did everything together...movies...ah...studying...everything."

"So he was over. Final tests of high school. So why not right? And Joanne – my wife Joanne – asked me to go call them to dinner. I should've knocked on the door before I opened it. I really should've. I know that. I've looked at that moment ever since. And I see it so clearly...Except why...And there they were...no shirts...Joe is on top of the other boy...their mouths on each other. And they saw me – or heard me because I may have made a sound – and got up. And Larry or Gary or whatever puts on his shirt. And excuses himself and leaves. And Joe says nothing. And won't look at me. And I say to him...I say...YOU. ARE. NOT. MY SON."

And Raymond broke. Something deep in the middle cleaved in two and he bent over into himself. He cried, long drawn-out sounds so low in his throat that it sounded like it was pushing something out on top of it. And his voice, the sound of it stretched and cracked and shattered into pieces, drifted out over the top of it.

"You're not my son. That's what I sad."

A breeze picked up and carried the sentence out into the wind. And yet the sound remained, weaving in and around the old man and the sobbing. Raymond was exhausted and couldn't breathe and yet he couldn't stop either. He heard Bill start to move by his side – he was there after all. The rubbing and bouncing would start and then stop, followed by guttural mumbling, before starting up again. He sounded upset by the story Raymond hadn't meant to tell. But it wasn't done yet.

Raymond took one long sigh. His voice still sounded jagged as he spoke again. "That was the last time I saw Joe. With the red marks of my fingers across his face. Because I...I hit him. Never before or since, but that night I did." He looked over at Bill who tried to make eye contact and then looked away.

"He was gone the next morning when we got up. No one knew where he was. Imagine going to graduation hoping to see your son as he walks across the stage. But he wasn't there. We didn't know what to do. We went to the police but he was eighteen so he could do what he wanted. Which was be away from me."

"Finally, one day, the doorbell rang. It was Larry or Gary. He had heard from him. He was in a place called Ft. Gordon, Georgia. He joined the army. Joe. Who never wanted to be a farmer. Now wanted to be a soldier. So he could fight back?"

It was becoming harder and harder to speak. But the words were pushing themselves out so he had no choice but to continue Bill was starting to mumble and the rhythm of that seemed to go with Raymond's words as he continued.

"Of course we wrote to him. Of course no answer. Then the doorbell rang again. Weeks later. I thought that was something they only did in the movies. Come to the door to tell you..." Raymond paused and in the pause a sound escaped his throat. "To tell you your son is gone. There was an accident. At least they called it an accident. In the barracks. But there were bruises. On his neck. When they shipped him back." Raymond was crying again. "My boy...my boy was gone." He heard the words as if for the first time. "My boy...He was my boy."

Overhead a seagull made a calling sound. He looked up and saw it moving across the sky until he had to squint into the sun and then he looked away. His hands were shaking and he held them together to calm them. A sigh filled him and left him. He felt so tired. He didn't know if he could ever move again.

"He...he died." A statement, not a question, floated out of the sounds Bill was making. With an enormous effort Raymond turned his head to look at the veteran.

"Yes, he..."

"Nonononononononono. He didn't he didn't no no, no he didn't no..." The words came out of Bill in a fast jabbing torrent of sound. He turned to the old man and thrust his whole body in front of Raymond, so close that the old man could smell his breath. "Nononononononono please nononono. Please no. He didn't. He didn't. He didn't." The torrent of words got louder and louder.

And then his hands were on the lapels of Raymond's sweater and was shaking him and the old man's hands flew up to protect himself, his cane clattering to the ground. Raymond pushed himself away but Bill held on and continued to shake them both and Raymond lost his balance and fell off the bench and Bill followed after and on top of him and the litany of "No's" continued and Raymond's voice joined Bill's saying "No! Please! Stop!" and Bill was gripping Raymond's head in his hands and Raymond's head was raising off the sidewalk and he was reaching up to try and swing at Bill's face but could not connect because there was so much movement and the "No" was just sound but it sounded like "Joe" and then it became "Joe" and Raymond heard himself cry out "Joe please don't hurt me!"

And in that moment Bill jerked his head up and froze and Raymond's fingers slid through the dog tag chain around Bill's neck and pulled forward with more strength than he knew he had. The chain broke and slid down onto Raymond' face but the dog tags were gripped in his fist.

And suddenly Bill was off Raymond and up in the air. A pair of muscular arms, brown and veiny, were wrapped around the veteran's waist and hurled him a short distance away on to the sidewalk. He crumpled onto the concrete making soft whining sounds. Over him towered a massive black man, tall and solid, surrounded by light. He was literally blocking the sun. He held his fists, gnarled and round like rocks, in front of him like a boxer as he approached the man cowering on the ground.

"What the hell's wrong with you? Attacking a defenseless old man! Why, I should beat you..." He bent down so that he could look Bill in the eyes. "You want me to call the cops? Huh? Do you?" Bill scrambled to his feet and backed away from the big man, who stood again to his full height. "No don't. Please don't." Bill waved his hands in front of him as if to erase the black man, who only laughed. "Get out of here, you piece of shit." His teeth flashed white as he spoke. But Bill stayed frozen to the spot. The big man stamped his foot, which seemed to unfreeze Bill – he turned and scurried down the sidewalk, the same hitch in his walk doing double time as he went. "Yeah you better get out of here you motherfucker!" the black man shouted after him.

Then he turned back to Raymond, who had managed to sit up and lean against the bench. But instead of puffing himself up and growling like he did with Bill, he crouched down in front of the old man, soft and gentle and quiet. "Raymond, is that you?" he asked.

Raymond searched his face. "There are people out there looking for you." The big man continued. Raymond took off his glasses and ran his hand across his forehead. His head hurt and, despite his best efforts, his heartbeat wouldn't slow back down. He felt the other man's hands on his shoulders and he flinched before he could stop himself. "I get it," he heard the other man say. "He roughed you up pretty good. Though I will say..." He took Raymond's chin in one hand and moved it from side to side. "I don't see any real damage." This was starting to feel familiar to Raymond. A big man with a soft touch. And it was a recent memory – that he was sure of. He pulled his head away and put his glasses back on. The black man got on his feet and held his hand out to Raymond. "Maybe I should take you back to the hospital to have you checked out."

Raymond looked up at the other man. He was blocking the sun again. Back to the hospital. Where he went seemingly healthy and left with cancer. Where he fell and a man with muscles picked him up and carried him.

"I remember you," Raymond said slowly. "Yeah. It's me." Bennie smiled. "Good. That's a good sign. You're back with us again. Well, I promised your daughter that once I left work and went to my second job that I would keep my eye out for you." He stepped to one side and sunshine hit Raymond's face, though he could still see a taxi idling at the curb. Bennie stepped back in front of the sun and held out his hand.

"So...how about we get you up off the ground first and then decide what to do with you?" Raymond nodded, but as he reached for his cane he saw other things on the ground as well. He had dropped the bouquet when he'd fallen to the ground and petals of many colors were scattered around it. In among the petals were other things – a plastic giraffe, a sleeve of chocolate wafers (surprisingly, still sealed, though the cookies inside were somewhat the worse for wear), a torn religious pamphlet. In his hand he still clutched Bill's dog tags. He dropped them into the pocket of his sweater before picking the other items up slowly one at a time.

"What you got there?" Bennie asked.

Just some...some things I picked up along the way," Raymond replied without looking up. He picked up the bouquet, which was still held together at the stems by a ribbon, and held his hand out to be helped up. Bennie's grip was strong enough to break bones, but he pulled slowly without jerking and Raymond was on his feet in one fluid movement. His cane dropped to the ground again and Bennie bent over to pick it up and handed it back to Raymond.

Raymond could count on one hand the number of times he had ridden in a cab. Each time the taxi had a distinct smell. Cigarettes. Fried food. One even smelled like someone had thrown up. Bennie's cab smelled like flowers. He had offered to let the old man sit in the front seat with him but Raymond preferred all the space in the back seat, so Bennie got him settled in and jumped behind the wheel, his seat practice-ally wheezing with the effort of taking all of Bennie's mass at one time. He looked in the rearview mirror at Raymond.

"So...I really think we should take you to the hospital. Just to get you looked at. See if there's any damage."

"No." Raymond shook his head. He was so worn out it felt as if he were sinking into the upholstery. "I was just there. Don't want to go back." He shook his head again. "I know there's
damage."

"Oh?" Bennie turned around on that, though one look at Raymond's face told him what he meant. "Oh. Okay. Well where would you like me to take you? Your daughter maybe? I know she's worried about you."

"I know she is." Raymond nodded his head. But something had caught his eye, a book wedged between the seats in the front. He could almost read the spine of the book, so he reached forward to lift it up and look at it. Bennie shrugged. "A fare left that in the car. I was starting to read it. But you can have it if you want."

It was "Farewell My Lovely" by Raymond Chandler. The book that was on the shelf in the room where his mother was giving birth. The book that gave him his name. "Yes. Yes I would like it. If you don't mind."

"Knock yourself out," Bennie said. "So

where are we headed?"

"Wait," Raymond said. He dug his wallet out of his pocket and pulled out the piece of paper with the number and address written by his grandson. When the old man said the address, Bennie's eyes shot up. "Huh...that's literally right around the corner." He turned to face forward and put the car into gear. Raymond could see Bennie's eyes looking at him in the rearview mirror. "You're almost made it home Raymond."

Literally was right. Bennie drew north two blocks, turned right, drove down one block and turned left at a street made of dark brick. The ride was bumpier on brick but Bennie slowed the cab to a crawl as he checked the numbers on the houses to his left. About halfway down he stopped the cab at the curb, jumped out and opened the back door to help Raymond. "We have arrived good sir." Bennie smiled as he said that, almost bowing to Raymond once the old man stood in front of him. Raymond tipped his head in return. Just then the dispatch went off in cab, informing Bennie of a fare.

'Listen," he said. "You got it from here? I mean, I could help you to the door if you want..."

Raymond waved him away. "Nah. I've got it from here." He held out his hand to Bennie, who shook it. So gently. "Thank you so much," Raymond said, "for getting me home."

"My pleasure. Anytime." Benny turned and walked to the cab but looked back one more time after he opened the door. "Tell Cassie hello for me." He smiled again and winked. "She seemed nice, your daughter."

Raymond stood on the sidewalk and watched the cab until it turned the corner and was gone from view. What a good man Bennie was. Raymond was really sorry he had to lie to him. One more thing he would have to ask forgiveness for he figured. And Bennie was right about Cassie. She was nice. She just needed time to figure it out. He had a feeling she would like Bennie too, if given half a chance.

He turned to look at the house. The front door was exactly in the center of the front with a window on either side. It looked like a nose and eyes. The house had a face and it was looking at him, though not unkindly. There were three steps leading up to a covered porch. He felt so tired. And it felt as if Bill was still pressing down on his chest. But he had come so far. He was almost home. He took the steps one at a time and rang the doorbell. He could hear it echo on the inside of the house, but no other sound. He rang the bell again, and suddenly there were footsteps. The door opened with a whoosh that seemed to pull all of the air off the porch and into the house.

It had been years since he had seen her. But to Raymond she looked exactly the same.

"Oh Ray," Joanne said.

So today it was just Ray.

CHAPTER 13

Once Joey was old enough to use large words, he would refer to the closets in their house as "archeological digs." And she would threaten to snatch him bald-headed – which she would never do because that was his father's hair, Dwight's hair, who smoked too much and died a year ago – and he would run screaming from the room and she would follow him, or at least pretend to. It was kind of their thing. But now, standing in front of the closet in her bedroom with the door open, she saw what he meant. There was fresh shit on the top, but the farther down she got there was absolutely no telling what brand of subterranean critters she would even encounter should she care to look. The whole thing was piled so high that it touched the edges of the shirts that hung there. Long ago she had moved what few dresses she still fit into the hall closet. She saw the big round letters of her mother's print on some of the boxes CASSIE'S SCHOOLWORK for example. She was always so good about trying to keep track. But there were things in here in plastic grocery bags, and after a while she didn't even do that. Things brushed up against the shirts that were simply haphazard piles.

But now was the time. She hadn't heard from the police yet and she needed something to not think about. Besides, she was tired. Tired of being angry and mean. Tired of being tired. She needed to not be those things. Her mother, in a fit of frustration about the condition of her room in her teen years, would say "some of your things need a good throwing away." Well right now some of her life needed a good throwing away. A wiping clean as it were. Stop carrying all the things. Looking at the smudges. And then go from there.

The waste basket from under the sink filled quickly at first. She emptied repeatedly. Whole stacks of paper knocked in with one sweep of the hand. Entire plastic bags picked up and dropped in the garbage. It was what she imagined a feeding frenzy would look like, blood and guts flying everywhere, except she was the single shark and all of this bullshit was the kill.

And then she started to slow down. She would find something, and seeing it would give her pause. A report card of Joey's from eighth grade. Why just one and not nine years of them she had no idea, especially since the grades on it were Bs and Cs and one D. A gift card to a restaurant she didn't remember using but definitely remembered getting. A rubber ball with dirty smudges on it. So she started a pile. Shit that Joey could have if he wanted. Shit she would hold onto herself and maybe be part of a scrapbook someday. Do people even do scrapbooking anymore she wondered as she thumbed through his sixth grade science notebook. Cursive was always a struggle for him and all of his notes were written in big round curvy print. His margins were filled with drawings of flowers and butterflies and hands and feet and faces. Of boys.

Always of boys.

She turned to drop the notebook onto the shit-Joey-might-want pile and heard sounds coming from the living room. Joey was watching TV, which was unusual for him. Usually if there was sound involved it was music and it was deep in his ears and not out in the air for the world to hear. She put the notebook on top of Joey's stack of stuff and trudged out of her bedroom and down the hall towards the sound. She was one of the few people she knew who still had a landline. Joey might not hear it over the TV and she wanted to get it right away in case the police called with news about her dad.

She started to speak as soon as she walked through the doorway – "Here. This shit is yours if you want it" was the most likely non-conversation-starter – when she saw the TV and stopped. He was watching cartoons. Wile E. Coyote was chasing after the Road Runner again and was strapping all kinds of crap to his feet and back – rockets, dynamite – in order to accelerate in his direction. Joey was stretched out the length of the couch in rapt attention. His feet were dangling over the arms. She took a few steps into the room and sat slowly down in a chair next to the couch, resting his stuff on her lap. She had watched these cartoons as a child and often would feel sorry for the coyote, worrying and fussing and crying that he would get hurt or that he could never get what he wanted. Now, however, as she watched in silence, the character just seemed like an asshole. Try to keep up with the fucking bird if that's what you want. Or find something else. Finally, after he'd gone off the cliff and a little white cloud from far away indicated he'd hit the ground, she looked over at her son. He was barely blinking at the screen. He hadn't even acknowledged she was there.

"Well listen," she began. "I decided it was time to purge a little bit. Get rid of some shit." The use of the curse word didn't even make him wince but she pushed a little. "But I found some stuff of yours. If you want it. I'm sure this is just a start. But I thought maybe…"

Joey's eyes flickered in her direction, flickered to the pile of stuff in her lap, and then back to the screen. "Sure Mom. That's fine. Just leave it right there and I'll take it to my room later."

She lifted his stuff a little off her lap and bounced it in the air as if she was weighing it. She got no response. So much talk earlier in the day and now this. She plowed on. "Okay. You haven't heard the phone ring have you? I'm a little worried about your grandpa."

"I'm sure he's fine Mom. They'll call us if they find out anything."

"Oh I know. It's just…I can't imagine where a seventy-eight year old man could have gotten himself off to. I mean, I wonder what possessed him to just up and leave the waiting room like that."

A slight flicker of the eyes, the long lashes down and then back up, and she realized she's said something.

"I don't know Mom. It's Grandpa. You know how he is."

"I know. I just don't want him to get hurt. He's old and he's not doing well. He can't take care of himself like he used to."

Another flicker, and his eyes darted in her direction before returning to the TV. "They'll call us when they know something. You know they will." He said to the cartoon.

"I know. I know. Sorry I just..." She sighed heavily as she put the stack on the floor beside the chair. "I mean, did he have some place he wanted to go? Or is he just out there walking around. I just...I don't know..."

That did it. His hand shot out to the coffee table in front of him and grabbed his cell phone. He instantly moved his thumbs across the keys and began to scroll through the screens.

"Joey," Cassie sat upright. "Do you know something?" No response, though his head bent closer to the phone.

"Joey?"

No response.

"Joey? What have you done?"

"Mom I..."
Just then the doorbell rang.
It was Bennie.

CHAPTER 14

"Oh Ray," Joanne said.

So today it was just Ray.

"May I come in?" He asked, gesturing into the house with the hand holding the mutilated bouquet. She pointed at it.

"What – did you bring me flowers?" She made a noise that sounded like a chuckle that died on the vine.

"Yes." Raymond smiled. "I suppose I did." He tried again. "So may I come in?" She touched her hair. Raymond thought women did that only in the movies. "Oh yeah. Sure. Sorry I..." She stepped aside and held her hand out to the house. "Sure. Please. Come in."

He stepped across the threshold into the living room. There were windows and light everywhere – the room ran the length of the house and the furniture looked soft and comfortable. Without thinking he moved his elbow out away from his body and she slipped her hand through and wrapped her fingers around his arm. The touch was there and so was the TV and the Sheriff and Miss Kitty and the couch in her parent's house and the first time their fingers came in contact. And all the fifty-five years since then.

    He hobbled with her through into the dining room and a table and six chairs. Once he got to the table he leaned against it a little and held the flowers out to her and smiled.

    "You have a vase for these?" He shook it a little and petals drifted to the hardwood floor. "Oh well..." She said and there was a bit of a laugh that time, a sound that wasn't stuck in her throat that time. He rested the bouquet on the table and his arm brushed against the bulging pocket of his sweater. "Ah. And..." He reached in and pulled out his gifts from Adam and Liv and Mike and Bill and Bennie. He arranged them across the tabletop and Joanne studied them for a minute and re-arranged them until they were in a straight line in front of them. They both looked at them until Joanne said, almost in a whisper, "Look. It's a life."

    And it was:

    A toy from a baby

Wafers from a child
Dog tags from a soldier
Flowers from a wedding
Do You Believe?
Farewell My Lovely

"Yes it is. It is indeed." He said it as much to himself as to anyone. He looked at her and she was already looking at him, her eyes wet. They held the look before Raymond looked away and ran one hand across his forehead.

"I'm really. Tired. Do you think I could…?"

"Oh sure. I'm sorry. Here. Let's sit down." She took his arm again and steered him back into the living room to an overstuffed brown chair. "And water? Do you think I could have some water?" He asked once he'd been seated. "I walked quite a ways to get here."

"Sure. Be right back." And she was gone, perhaps a little faster than was absolutely necessary. It was when she walked away that Raymond noticed her dress had flowers on it.

He looked around the room as he waited. Small but not tight. Cozy he thought the word might be. Big windows with lots of mid-day light coming through. Couch, chairs, TV, all the usual. Fireplace on one end. Ceiling fans rotating slowly. And it smelled good, like clothes that had been hanging in the summer sun. The chair he sat in almost seemed to envelope him. He felt like he could stay there forever.

She was back by his side handing him the water. A glass, with water from the tap probably, instead of a plastic bottle from the refrigerator. She sat on the edge of the sofa and faced him as he gulped the water, tilting the glass up as far as he could until it was all gone. He imagined the water seeping through the fingers of the disease wrapping itself around his insides. She reached over and took the glass and put it on the coffee table. She was watching him closely Raymond thought. She seemed calmer then when he'd first surprised her. He listened to the fans as they rotated above him and tried to attach an emotion to the situation. Anger didn't stick because there was none there. And he was all out of sadness – had been, he thought, for quite some time and simply living on crumbs. The best he could come up with was relief, like a jump in the heart when something was finally and forever finished. He smiled at her without speaking.

"I have thought about this moment for some time," she said finally. "Thought about what I would say. I would lie in bed and rehearse one thing. And then another. And another. And...I just..."

"Joanne, I'm sick."

"What?" Something flickered across her face.

"Sick. I'm real sick." He knew there were more words. But he saw she understood.

"How...How long?"

He started and then stopped and then started again. "Ahh...a little while."

"Oh." A shadow moved across her face again. He wanted so much to reach out and take her hand – the touch again, so important – but the couch seemed so far away. She wiped her hands under her eyes.

"How did you find me?" She sniffled as she spoke.

"Your grandson. Did you know you have a grandson?"

"Uh...yeah. Yes I did actually."

"What?" This stopped him.

"Joey. Joseph. Cassie named him after her brother."

"But how...?" Raymond was suddenly very confused. Joanne sighed, a sound so deep it seemed to come from way back in the past.

"Oh Ray." At least he was still Ray. "There is so much I need to say." She paused for a moment and swallowed before she began. "Our son died. I know you think it was your fault somehow, that the fight you had with him beforehand made everything else fall into place. And it was sad. So sad. More sad than I could handle, really. And the truth of the matter was, if I couldn't handle my own sadness than could I handle yours as well? And you were crushed... absolutely...devastated." She paused. "It was 'Stop! I'm drowning here already! You're killing me. Literally killing me with your sorrow.' And I was so tired. Tired of holding on to everything so tight and it still didn't do any good and now all I was holding onto was air. Everything hurt. Hurt so much...So I just. Let. Go." Her hands had become fists as she talked, so tight the knuckles were white, but she opened them wide. "And you let me go. Because it was the same for you. I didn't even have to leave while you were away. You were there." She rested her hands in her lap. "And I lived someplace else and thought I'd call once I got settled in. And I got settled. And I didn't call, but kept thinking I would."

"And then you called. But there was so much silence over the phone. And the one thing that's almost as bad as sadness is silence. And the two together..." She shook her head. She sat there for a minute, looking as tired as Raymond felt. But she continued.

"I became a nurse. And bought a house. And made a life. And waited for the hurt to be less."

She shifted in her seat. "So much of what went on after isn't worth talking about. It was just time... And then one day Cassie finds me. You know how it is in this day and age. They go on their computers and type in a name and find someone in minutes..."

"I know. That's how Joey found you."

"Joey did?"

"Yeah. He spends so much time looking at his phone. One day I just asked him if he could look up people on that thing, since he was looking up music. He looked at me real funny when I said the last name. But he found you." Raymond licked his lips. He probably needed more water. "I probably shoulda told him you were his grandma."

Joanne shook her head. "No no. I get it. Cassie and I talked about that when we finally talked. He already had a relationship with you..."

Raymond laughed. "Yeah. A six-word-a-day relationship."

Joanne joined him. "Yeah, but it was a relationship. It seemed so...I don't know... complicated to add me to the mix. We thought about waiting until he was older and let him decide for himself. But I couldn't help myself. There was a daughter. And a grandson. So at some point I moved. To be close by. Just in case."

"How much older were you going to let him get?"

She shook her head again. "I know. I know. I don't know. Like you said. Shoulda. You shoulda maybe not yelled at your son so that it sent him off to the army. I shoulda maybe stayed with you so we could try and find a way through this together. Maybe I shoulda gotten to know our grandson. Maybe we shoulda held onto our only surviving child so she maybe wouldn't wind up an angry old lady."

"She isn't old. She'd still got time. We're the old ones."

Joanne smiled and touched her grey hair. "That certainly is the truth right there."

"Plus," he continued. "She's got Joey."

"What's he like? Our grandson?" She asked.

He thought for a moment. "Quiet. Real good-looking. Almost pretty. Lots of hair. Seems real smart. He may figure it out before any of the rest of us."

It was quiet in the house then. Raymond closed his eyes and listened to the fan blades overhead. That's all there was at that moment. He could no longer imagine a disease with long fingers squeezing his insides. He no longer had difficulty breathing. He felt light, almost like he was made out of nothing but air. He felt as if he could stay in this chair, kin this house, forever. He heard movement and opened his eyes. Joanne was kneeling in front of him. "Our little boy got lost Raymond," she said slowly. "And then we got lost because we couldn't find him. I am so sorry I didn't come find you before now." She paused and sniffled. Her eyes were wet again. "But it's okay. You're home now. You're home with me."

Raymond reached out and touched her face. "You say lost like he's out there somewhere waiting to be found."

She wiped her face with the back of her hand. "He is." She stood in front of him and held out her hand. "I want to show you something."

There was no tugging as he stood. He barely felt as if he needed his cane. They went back over the threshold, out onto the porch and down the steps onto the sidewalk. Her arm was cradled in his. That touch. Across the street was a brick wall that ran most of the length of the street. She steered him to the left, still heading north. Farther down the block was an archway and an open gate. They turned into the cemetery walked down a sidewalk with rows of graves on either side. Just after passing a gazebo, Joanne stopped and turned and pointed. In front of them was an expanse of grass with a single tombstone several steps away. He let go of her arm and hobbled over to read the inscription.

    Joseph Dale Chandler
    1967-1985
    Beloved Son

    He stood for a long time looking down at the stone. The last two words were all he could see. Joanne walked up behind him. "I moved him here," she said. "When my dad died he left me some money. And I spent it on this." She gestured to the ground around her. "There is space for you. And me. And Cassie and Joey if they want it. There's room for all of us."

    Raymond's eyes stung. His throat felt dry and he couldn't swallow. His hands were trembling and he dropped his cane. Joanne sat on the stone and patted beside her. "Here, Ray, why don't you sit down." But instead he bent down, got to his hands and knees and sat on the ground. Underneath was his son and he was safe. Raymond would make sure of that. He lay his head in

Joanne's lap. He reached down to him and touched his hair.

"Welcome to the day Ray," she said, almost in a whisper. "Welcome home."

Off in the distance he heard voices. He turned his head and saw three figures entering the cemetery. No doubt the cab driver/hospital aide had realized he didn't take Raymond to his daughter's house and went to fetch her. He looked back up at this wife who was looking down at him smiling. He felt so light. He was no longer heading towards the horizon. Rather, the horizon was heading towards him. So fast. He could go to sleep here so easily. He continued looking up at her. Her head was backlit by clear blue cloudless sky. And he knew, like he had understood his whole life but had just now slipped into knowing.

He knew what color her eyes were.

They were blue. Like the sky.

Like heaven.

Made in the USA
Columbia, SC
04 June 2021